# THOSE FANTASTIC LIVES

## AND OTHER STRANGE STORIES

# THOSE FANTASTIC LIVES

### AND OTHER STRANGE STORIES

## BRADLEY SIDES

A City of Light Publishing imprint

Blacklight Press
A City of Light imprint

City of Light Publishing
266 Elmwood Ave. Suite 407
Buffalo, New York 14222

info@CityofLightPublishing.com
www.CityofLightPublishing.com

Book design by Ana Cristina Ochoa

ISBN 978-1-952536-20-5 (softcover)
ISBN 978-1-952536-21-2 (eBook)

10 9 8 7 6 5 4 3 2 1


Library of Congress Cataloging-in-Publication Data:
Names: Sides, Bradley, author.
Title: Those fantastic lives : and other strange stories / Bradley Sides.
Description: Buffalo, New York : Blacklight Press, a City of Light imprint, [2021] | Summary: "Prepare
    to be transported to the edge of the world in Bradley Sides' affecting and haunting debut collection
    of magical realism short stories, Those Fantastic Lives and other strange stories. In Sides' tender,
    brilliantly-imagined collection, a young boy dreams of being a psychic like his grandmother, a
    desperate man turns to paper for a miracle, a swarm of fireflies attempts the impossible, scarecrows
    and ghosts collide, a mother and child navigate a forest plagued by light-craving monsters, a boy's
    talking dolls aid him in conquering a burning world, and a father and mother deal with the sudden
    emergence of wings on their son's back. Brimming with our deepest fears and desires, Sides' dazzling
    stories examine the complexities of masculinity, home, transformation, and loss. Bradley Sides is
    an exciting new voice in fiction, and Those Fantastic Lives, which glows with the light of hope and
    possibility amidst dark uncertainties, will ignite imaginations"-- Provided by publisher.
Identifiers: LCCN 2021033212 (print) | LCCN 2021033213 (ebook) | ISBN 9781952536205 (trade
    paperback) | ISBN 9781952536212 (ebook) | ISBN 9781952536212 (epub) | ISBN 9781952536212
    (kindle edition) | ISBN 9781952536212 (mobi) | ISBN 9781952536212 (pdf)
Subjects: LCGFT: Short stories.
Classification: LCC PS3619.I345 T48 2021  (print) | LCC PS3619.I345
    (ebook) | DDC 813/.6--dc23
LC record available at https://lccn.loc.gov/2021033212
LC ebook record available at https://lccn.loc.gov/2021033213

*For all the dreamers,*
*young and old—those now and those becoming...*

# CONTENTS

# THOSE FANTASTIC LIVES

**O**NE MISTAKE IS WHAT SEPARATED Nellie from the others—the "fakies" as she called them. Nellie was no Miss Francine, and she certainly wasn't a part of the, even worse, Psychic Sisters Network. She told her eight-year-old grandson, Sam, to mute the television every time one of the Psychic Sisters' cheap ads came blaring from the screen. Those old ladies and their stupidly-written, synchronized sentences. As if completing someone's thought was enough to make a person a psychic—or any kind of clairvoyant for that matter. "Please," she grunted to Sam, rolling her eyes. "Those women wouldn't know a real psychic if one bit them on their collective behind."

Nellie conducted her last session before her self-imposed retirement no differently than the hundreds of others that had come before. Sure, she was admittedly a lot slower answering the door than the first time she'd welcomed a customer, but she still wore the same padded slippers to do so. Her familiar beige gown with faded black roses swept across the carpet the same way it always had, and, when she reached for the doorknob, her hands still first had to fumble with her antique celestial headwrap in an effort to contain the graying hairs sprouting from beneath its edges. These were Nellie's ways.

"Moira!" she announced before she'd even fully opened the door. She extended her arms to the young woman on her steps. Moira, with her perfect skin and shiny black hair, shyly stepped back and put out her hand to shake Nellie's.

"I knew it was you before I ever saw you. I'm the real thing, you know," Nellie said, trying too hard for even herself.

"You already know my name. I have an appointment."

"Relax. It's just a little psychic humor. Besides, I'm a psychic. I'm not in the fortune-telling business," Nellie said. Moira smirked.

For a moment, Nellie was quiet, fidgeting with her rings. "You are even more beautiful than I imagined," she soon said, shifting the conversation in a more cordial direction. Her body loosened when she saw Moira's reaction.

The woman's face relaxed at the compliment, and her crooked teeth gleamed in the morning sunlight.

Nothing could last forever, though. The smell of cigarettes and baby powder seeped out of the doorway and blanketed Moira. She fanned the air and spit into the sky. "Thank you," she choked out, unable to ignore the compliment.

"Come, baby. Come. You are my last reading in this lifetime, so let's get going. I have a retirement to enjoy," Nellie said amidst her own episode of sputtering, damp coughs.

The two women regained their composure. Then, Nellie stepped outside and grabbed her new client by the arm. "Come on," she said.

When they were inside, she slammed the door shut.

Nellie ushered Moira down the hallway, past the dusty black and white photographs of her deceased family members. She pointed to each one. "That one's thriving on the other side. This one is busy. And this one is very, very wild. You wouldn't believe it." She turned to Moira and winked.

Nellie stopped and stood at a portrait of her grandmother. She held her hand to her chest. "I miss this one the most, but she's happy—just like she was in life," Nellie said. "He," she said, flinging her arm up to the picture of her grandfather, "well, let's just say that he's not." Nellie chuckled before she quickly grimaced and shook her head.

"Oh," Moira said as her eyes widened.

"Loosen up, girl. Don't be so nervous," Nellie said. "I'll get you your answers. I'm not one of those fakies."

Nellie led Moira into the reading room and pulled out a large wooden chair from the circular table. "Please," she said, motioning for Moira to sit.

The customer obliged. Her eyes traveled around the strange room. The midnight-colored ceiling. The scarlet, silk-draped walls. The candles on the edges of the floor. The crystal ball on the table. It looked ridiculous. Nellie knew as much; she hated it herself. But she didn't have much of a choice if she wanted to compete against the fakies and their entire faux "medium" lives that popular culture had concocted and which had, consequently, tarnished the entire psychic community's once serious reputation since the '90s. Colors. Candles. Crystal balls. Customers expected it. All of it.

Nellie, though, didn't need anything other than a spirit—although, at her age, she did appreciate a sturdy chair. She could reach voices at the supermarket while waiting on her turkey to be sliced if she needed.

She moved to the other side of the cherry table and sat across from Moira. Nellie took a moment to collect her breath, and she wiped the streams of sweat that ran from her forehead and down her neck. She closed her eyes.

"Do you need me to get you some water or something?" Moira asked.

Nellie shook her head and looked up. "Are you ready to begin?"

Moira readjusted in her seat. "Is this going to hurt?"

"Hurt?" Nellie asked. "No, girl. This won't hurt." She stared at Moira, who didn't seem very comforted. "Why?" Nellie followed up. "Did you think it was going to hurt? Did someone tell you it might hurt? Did you hear it on one of those fakie Psychic Sisters' shows?"

"No, no," Moira said, her eyes peering up from her thick, magenta-rimmed glasses. "It's not that. I've just never done anything like this."

Nellie wiggled her shoulders. "Oh, I see. No pain involved. Just relax." Nellie clinched her hands and popped her knuckles. Her shoulders still danced about as she turned her head from side to side. "All ready," she said.

She draped her hands over the crystal ball, holding her palms out.

"Okay," Moira said hesitantly.

"Place your hands under mine," Nellie said, moving to the front of her chair.

Moira slowly extended her hands to the table.

"Come on. You can do it," Nellie said.

Moira sighed and gave Nellie her hands.

"Good. Now, just relax."

Moira closed her eyes and breathed deeply. She moved her weight to the back of her chair, and she listened.

A blanket of silence suffocated the room. The flames from the candles popped, and wax slithered down into the candles' cool holders. Each breath from the two women held power. Each soul drifting away into grayness, but, still, their bodies present—both searching.

Nellie's mouth began to open. Slowly at first and then wider. Her throat loosened. Sounds gurgling. Sounds building. Sounds trying to break free.

Moira opened her eyes, and she watched Nellie. She'd heard that each psychic had her own way of contacting the other side. She wanted to see Nellie's.

The psychic's eyes rolled back into her head and her entire body shook as her mouth summoned a soul.

"Jackson?" Moira whispered. "Are you here?" she asked.

Nellie's body violently convulsed. Then, the candles snuffed out. Her body was still.

"Are you here, son?" Moira asked.

"Mommy," a soft voice said.

"Jackson," she said. Her voice quivering. "Are you okay? Are you okay, baby?"

A rumbling interrupted the silence. The table rocked until it crashed, and a pair of small, bare feet rubbed against Moira's. They ran to the door and, then, through to the light in the hallway.

"Jackson!" Moira cried. She leapt from the table and chased the body that had escaped the room.

"Jackson!" her voice echoed down the hall and outside into the yard. "Jackson! Jackson!"

The inside of the reading room was quiet again. "Mommy?" the tender voice called.

A few seconds passed. "Mommy?" the voice asked.

But there was no answer.

Nellie dialed Moira a dozen times from her bed the next day to apologize, but each ring led to her voicemail—one with an impersonalized, computer-generated voice. There was no use, but Nellie still spoke at the command of the tone. She regretted what had happened. She was sorry. She was sorry. She was sorry.

But her apology wasn't totally sincere. She hadn't failed in the reading. Jackson came through. Nellie felt him. Moira spoke to him. He was in the room.

It was Sam who should be apologizing. Little Sam and his big curiosity.

Sam had lived with Nellie since he was three days old, and he'd grown up in her land of the dead. Her area of expertise wasn't a secret. She taught him about spirits and the other side. On his fourth birthday, she bought him—them—a Ouija board. She showed him how it worked and laughed when they "conjured" spirits he heard, which usually belonged to guinea pigs or unicorns. Sometimes, it was his father or his mother that he spoke to, but Nellie quickly corrected Sam during those moments. "They are not dead to the world, baby. Just to us."

He spied from his bedroom at Nellie's clients, but he never spoke to them. Nellie told him he was too young to be in the world of grown folks. "Little boys do little boy kinds of things," she said, but she never exactly explained what "little boy kinds of things" included.

He helped with just about everything. He seasoned the food she made, dried the dishes she washed, and folded the laundry she cleaned. All without complaint.

He kept Nellie's schedule, for her, in a notebook. When she hung up the phone, she told him what to write, and he did.

He questioned the empty dates, as they grew more and more. "Are we going on another trip, Nana?" he asked her.

"I'm too old for trips," she said.

She told Sam she was retiring and didn't say anything else. He would need to figure it out on his own, but he'd seen enough lunchtime soap operas to know what the word meant. Those same stories helped him understand a lot of what Nellie often talked about. But retiring—well, retiring was different. It was a word that didn't quite fit her.

Although Nellie advised him not to play with his Ouija board alone, that's exactly what he did on the morning of her final session. After he woke up Nellie as he usually did, an hour before her appointment, he went to his room and sat on the floor.

At eight, he was more serious with his efforts to connect with Nellie on her level. That desire to reach her increased by the day. He began to wear faded, wizard-like gowns and a coal black turban to breakfast. "And what is this?" she asked him.

"I'm going to be a psychic, too."

"Fine," she said, sipping her tea.

He was actually getting somewhere with his efforts. When he focused hard enough, the planchette slid over the board's letters without any extra assistance. Something else began to happen, too. He could hear whispers if the house was totally silent.

On the morning Moira arrived, Sam listened for half an hour to the board, finally hearing the name "Jackson."

The name meant nothing to him at that moment, but maybe it would to Moira, the final name Sam had written down in Nellie's schedule.

Sam's plan was in order. When Nellie went outside to greet Moira, he would slip from his bedroom and into the reading room, where he knew his grandmother would conduct the reading like she did all of her others. And he did.

He hid behind one of the curtains on the wall, but the shadows made his presence too obvious. The table was big enough to hide underneath. He ducked under the wooden surface and crouched against the center pedestal. When Nellie and Moira entered the room, he became like a statue. Still. Quiet.

As each chair moved, he pivoted. His body avoided contact, and he positioned himself against the table again. Nellie's shaking caused his body to loosen, but her actions weren't entirely unexpected. When she'd played with the Ouija board, she'd done the same.

He was fine until Moira said her son's name. At the announcement of "Jackson," he let out a gasp, but Moira was too focused to notice anything other than the words coming from Nellie's lips.

Sam had been right. He was hearing. He was connecting.

As Moira repeated her son's name, Sam couldn't contain his excitement. He fled.

Nellie waited until her stories were on before she said anything to Sam. The music swelled as the first scene, like most others, opened straight inside Lorraine's bedroom. Nellie was unusually grateful when one of her coughing episodes came. Her rattling blocked the seductive words from reaching Sam's ears.

When she finished, the scene continued, and it was getting worse. Everything was getting worse. She blurted, "Pause it! Pause it!" She flew up from the couch. "I can't take it!" she said.

"I don't want people thinking I'm one of those fakies. You know that. I'm Nellie. I'm not Miss Francine. And you know I'm for sure not one of those Psychic Sisters. You know this, Sam. You know it! You know it!" she said, with her voice rising with each sentence.

She continued, quicker, "I'm not a fakie! I've gone sixty-some years of reading after reading with no complications. None at all. I'm talking total perfection. I'm good, Sam. I've avoided all of the mumbo jumbo nonsense except for that hideous room. And now, what will become of my legacy? I'll just be one of them."

She, out of breath, sat back down, and dust blew from the couch cushions.

"I'm sorry, Nana, but I was excited," Sam said, putting the remote down.

"Yes, and nosy. Very, very nosy. What do I always tell you? Little boys do little boy kinds of things," Nellie said, her hands reaching for her pack of cigarettes. "I'm sorry," she whispered. "But I've got to have two."

Sam sighed. "Your doctor said you have to stop doing that," he said.

"Do I look like I care what my doctor said?"

Sam ignored her. "I'm not so little," he said.

"Eight *is* little."

"But I'm psychic, Nana. I'm like you."

"Blah, blah, blah," she said, lighting her smokes. "Your hands moved on a Ouija board."

"No," he corrected. "I heard a voice while I was using the Ouija board."

"It doesn't matter. That doesn't make you psychic."

"It might," he said.

Nellie turned her head up to the ceiling and puffed. Thick smoke covered the room. She took another taste from her double cigarette. "Did you at least tell Moira that you were sorry?" she asked quietly.

Sam's mouth turned crooked. "I tried, but she was crying too hard, and she slammed her car door in my face."

Nellie shook her head.

"You could come out of retirement," Sam suggested, leaning over to her and resting his head on her lap. "Maybe she'll agree to another reading."

"Not now," Nellie told him. "Just hit play." She didn't tell him to cover his eyes.

———

Sam waited a week before he called Moira. Nellie told him that it was for the best, but that he'd have to call her eventually. She explained that it was his responsibility to apologize for upsetting Moira.

As he held the phone in his sweaty palms, the little device nearly slid right out. He shook so badly that he had to hang up and redial half a dozen times. He had a script in front of him. The voicemail would be enough time for him to say what he needed to say.

When Moira picked up on the third ring, Sam dropped the phone. It, like his plan itself, was broken. He reached down and fumbled with what remained intact, and when he held the speaker back up to his ear, she was still on the line.

"Um, hello," he said. "This is Sam—Sam, the little boy from Nellie's." His voice sputtered.

"I know who it is," she replied.

The line was quiet.

"I—um—I," Sam began, "I'm sorry. I didn't mean to scare you and all."

"You didn't scare me."

"Oh," he said. "I'm still sorry."

Both were quiet again. Then, Moira huffed, causing the speaker to crack. "You didn't scare me, Sam. You upset me," she said slowly. "But I forgive you."

"You do?" he asked, perking up.

"I do," she assured him. "But I was very, very upset. I think you can imagine why."

"I can," he said. "I really am sorry."

"Thank you for calling to say so."

"You're welcome." he said. "I called for another reason, too." His voice perked up. "Nana will do another reading for free tomorrow if you are willing to come back."

"Oh, she will?" Moira asked. "I thought she was retiring."

"She did. She's coming out of retirement for one reading only. She swears it'll be her last one for real this time," he said. Then, he continued, "I won't upset you this time."

"Okay. I think I will agree to that."

"Good. I'll put you down for nine o'clock tomorrow morning on Nana's schedule."

"Bye, Sam." she said. "And thank you for calling."

"You're welcome."

He hung up the phone and went to find Nellie. He had some persuading to do.

Sam waited until the very last credit rolled on Nellie's stories for the day before he asked her. Her answer came slowly because her coughing prevented her from getting many words out.

When she came to, her hand crept over to the table beside her end of the couch, and she grabbed a pack of cigarettes. She slapped the box down on her legs and peeled back the top. She retrieved two slim sticks.

"Just light them," she said.

The house was unusually quiet when morning arrived. No snoring. No rustling. No pages turning. Being a boy raised on the importance of ritual, Sam still waited until an hour before Nellie's appointment with Moira before he went into his grandmother's bedroom.

When he turned the doorknob and pushed back the door, he didn't even have to go to her to know.

He ran to his room and grabbed the Ouija board from his toy shelf, ripping the box open and throwing the board onto the cold floor. His hands gripped the planchette as he closed his eyes. "Nana!" he cried. "Nana!"

The doorbell rang as his hands began to move, but Sam stayed on the floor. He focused on the board. "Nana!"

Then, the doorbell came again.

And again.

The sound echoed.

Sam took the planchette and threw it into the wall. He tore the board into pieces. It had always been only a game—just like Clue, but for dreamers.

"Nellie? Sam?" Moira called.

Sam closed his eyes, and he listened.

If she wouldn't come to him on the board, maybe she would come to him like Jackson had to her. He turned his head to the ceiling. He shook.

When he opened his eyes, Moira was standing in front of him—him with his swollen eyes, him with his broken heart.

She was crying, too.

He leapt from the floor and grabbed Moira's hand, hurrying her into the reading room.

He pulled out the same chair she'd sat in before, and she took it. He went to Nellie's.

When he held out his hands, Moira didn't hesitate.

They, as one, closed their eyes and searched—and they waited. They waited for those fantastic lives they loved to find them again.

When Sam came to, there was a woman in the doorway he recognized as the person he loved more than anyone. The same gown he'd seen her in so many times. The same headwrap that hid her age. But she wasn't alone. She was holding the hand of a little boy.

"I'm okay," the boy said. "Tell Mommy that I'm okay."

Sam squeezed Moira's hand, and she glanced up at him.

"I'm not a fakie," he whispered.

"What?" she asked, her tears falling onto the table.

He shook his head. He'd not meant to say it aloud.

"I can see him," Sam said, wiping away his tears. "He's okay."

"He's really okay?"

"And he will be," he said, looking back at Nellie.

Sam nodded at his grandmother, and they both smiled. Then, he turned back to Moira. He was ready for her next question.

# LOSING LIGHT

**B**EFORE.

All of us kids from the neighborhood were out in my front yard sitting and talking. Laughing and waiting. All but Gresh, that is. He, more than anybody, celebrated that first night of summer when the fireflies returned.

He howled as he ran in the yard. His bare feet smashed into the muddy puddles. Before even the tips of his toes could dry, he plowed into the rows of dandelions, pretending the white floaties were fireflies. Then, he fell into the dewy grass and the pieces of the world covered his body.

When they finally arrived, they bypassed the rest of us. Some of the younger kids called out and chased them, with their Mason jars clanking against their stubby, damp fingers. The rest of us already knew even if we wished we didn't.

The fireflies went toward Gresh. Their tiny bodies spun and sped. Flicked and glowed. Their lights were like a silent symphony—synchronized perfectly to create just what they'd intended.

Gresh didn't get up. He didn't speak. He didn't welcome them in any way. He just opened his mouth, and they found their way inside.

I couldn't watch for long. I said goodnight and went inside.

The others' voices followed me until I closed the door behind me, but they still played over in my head.

I peeked from my bedroom curtain one last time after I turned off my lamp. He was still out there. Glowing amidst all that darkness.

———

He sat at his little desk in silence most days, staring off into the sky. When the rest of us went swimming at the pool, he said he had important things to do if we asked if he wanted to go. But when night approached, he grew anxious. He tapped his feet against the wooden floor and he rocked back and forth in his chair. He slowly pecked at the window with his bitten fingernails.

When they inevitably returned, he howled with excitement and took off into the yard.

———

It was bad enough that I had a brother who housed thousands of bugs. It was even worse that he glowed. The worst, though, was how he sat in the front yard in the mornings with his little notebook and wrote away with nothing but the purely white tips of his glowing fingers. The neighbors used to call all the time and tell us about Gresh. He scared their kids, they said. Really, though, he scared them.

Mom constantly asked him what he was doing. He would always say the same thing: "Important stuff." When Dad asked him: "Important stuff." Me: "Important stuff." None of us knew what to say, so we didn't say anything.

One night when he was out illuminating the neighborhood, I went to his room and opened the notebook he'd been writing in all season. But, of course, there was nothing there I could see.

———

By the end of summer, I needed sunglasses if I was in the same room as Gresh. From underneath his clothes, you could see his bright body trying to find its place in a world it couldn't ever really belong in.

Although he glowed, he still looked dark around his eyes.

He didn't eat during the day. Mom and Dad worked. I played with my friends. He sat around and waited on his "friends."

Only a few fireflies remained on the night Gresh came to my bedroom and dropped the notebook on my bed. "Goodbye," he said. I nodded at him as I smirked.

I eventually looked out to see what he was doing—to see how many fireflies would find their way inside him—but when I opened my curtains, I couldn't see a thing. All of the light was gone.

FTER.

Even if I close my eyes and focus, I can't remember the way he smelled or the sound of his voice. But I can remember moments. There was that one day when his arm rubbed against me on his way to meet them one evening. He wasn't hot. He wasn't even warm. It was like that time he sliced his finger on the cover of one of my books he was returning, and he bled actual crimson blood. Honestly, I expected light. Bright, white light.

We still wait on their annual return. No one mentions Gresh to me, but I hear his name echoed in the soft breeze. The name engulfs and suffocates me. We all have Mason jars now. There's really not that much difference from the young and the old. We all want.

One of the kids trips over his shoelaces and falls. He rests on the ground and stares up at what surrounds him. He is quiet. It's like he's a part of a different world. It's brief, but it's gorgeous. I wonder if that's what Gresh felt all the time.

It really was beautiful if you think about it. The way those tiny, mysterious bugs flew to him with no effort on his part, and he allowed them inside him. To protect them? To comfort them? To befriend them? I just wish I knew why.

I wake up some mornings and wonder if Gresh was just a dream—if he was just someone we all made up in order to have something special in our lives. Then, I remember the laughter and the names. Some things can't be made up.

My parents are asleep, and my friends are at home. I peek outside from my window to watch them. It's what I do a lot of nights when I can't stop thinking about Gresh. Tonight, it's like I'm lost in space. The stars are twinkling. Bright then dark. Here then not. It's my whole unknown universe.

A firefly lands on my window, and its light dies.

I grab Gresh's notebook and go outside. The grass is cool when I sit down. The pages of his notebook float in the nighttime air. Unlike that night when I looked at the pages in his bedroom, there are words now here in the darkness. Or one word written over and over. His handwriting is heavy, frantic. "HELP!" There's something on one of my cheeks. Maybe it's a firefly. Maybe it's a tear.

I call his name. My voice is quiet at first, but it grows. "Gresh! Gresh!" The name feels strange coming from my mouth. I doubt I've said my brother's name more than a handful of times throughout my whole life, but it finds its place as I cry louder and louder.

I fall into the grass and look up at the bright dots burning above me. It's hard to focus. I can't tell the stars from the fireflies. I just know it's light. As long as it's here, I won't stop. I open my mouth, and I wait. I feel something on my lips. I can only hope I'm not too late.

It hits me. He was writing to them.

# BACK IN CROWVILLE

1. "What came first, the scarecrow or the town?" That's a joke people actually told in Crowville in the days before the Great Descension.

2. Worse than the joke itself was the fact that people found it funny—like laugh-out-loud funny.

3. Back then, the residents didn't laugh at much else.

4. Yeah, Crowville was one of those kinds of places.

5. Crowville was a small town. It was on maps and stuff, but when some ferocious hail from a surprise summer storm obliterated the town's sign, it didn't get replaced.

6. There were exactly 400 residents in total at the official count at the beginning of the decade. That number never changed much annually. A dozen or so babies arrived. A handful of people went off to college. A few croaked. The only real industry was scarecrow production. Pretty much all of the residents were a cog in that machine. Kids. Parents. Old

People. If you were a resident of Crowville and were capable of working a needle and thimble, you stitched scarecrows.

**7.** All I used to talk about was escaping as soon as I graduated. Could you blame me? Imagine you were in my shoes. Let's say at forty you are talking to your kid about all the things you used to do. For me, that would've been something like this: "Yeah, Dean Jr., I had a great life. The floor of my room was coated in cloth, twine, and stuffing, and I made the coolest little scarecrows. When my friends came over, we would sit around and talk about how awful everybody was as we were fighting over the different kinds of magic markers we might use for drawing the faces on the scarecrows we made with our own hands. Those were the good days, my man."

**8.** I don't think so.

**9.** As you can imagine, nobody visited Crowville. Or they didn't until…

**10.** The Great Descension.

**11.** The Great Descension was the greatest day of my life.

**12.** I'm not joking either. It was the literal greatest day of my entire existence. (I was still a virgin, mind you.)

**13.** Here's the gist of it all: early in the morning on this cloudy and drizzly day, the ground did a little rumble thing and then, light started falling from the sky. Flame-looking light. Orange. Red. Really, really bright, too. I thought it was fire, and I was good with that honestly. But it wasn't fire. The light was actually ghosts. Ghosts as in the returned dead. And ghosts were falling—or floating or flying—to earth. They had these transparent, glowing quasi-bodies and naked, flat faces. Hollowed eye sockets, but with a content smile. Silent things, too, like you'd expect. You could tell who they were because their shapes, clothes, and smells gave them away. Within five minutes, the population shot up to at least a thousand. Maybe five thousand. Or even ten. The point is that ghosts were everywhere. And they just floated around aimlessly. I went up to one and tried talking to it, but it didn't listen. I saw my grandmother and tried to give her a hug, but she just passed right through me. It was incredible.

**14.** It was also really, really entertaining. You might think a lot of people would be excited to see their loved ones again but trust me when I say they were not. The people of Crowville were FREAKED.

**15.** People were yelling and screaming. Like bloody murder screaming. They were yanking their kids by their shirts (or whatever else they could grab) and running to their houses. As soon as they got inside and slammed the door, they were zipping back on out to their porches and driveways. Like I said, the ghosts were everywhere, and they went right through roofs, walls, and everything else. It was like they saw the world as being empty.

**16.** I grabbed a lawn chair and sat in my front yard. People-watching had never been better.

**17.** "They were dying to get back to Crowville!" My joke. I yelled it as loudly as I could at the people running down the street.

**18.** I told a slightly different version to a ghost. It was something like this: "Hey, I bet you were dying to come back." The ghost took it about as well as the human, which means it didn't even acknowledge me.

**19.** All of the retail businesses, which were, for real, two Dollar stores, a one-pump gas station, and a scarecrow-themed consignment shop, closed for the day. The TV went to static. Nothing on the radio. Except for the constant howls of terror, Crowville was quiet. It was like we were living in a ghost town.

**20.** Ha!

**21.** During the evening of the Great Descension, Dad called an emergency family meeting, which meant he got to stand at the head of the dining room table and tell my mom, brother, and me, as we were sitting, what to do. Years of training meant that we nodded and didn't ask questions.

**22.** It also meant we didn't do anything he suggested.

**23.** For the record, he wanted us to wrap our bodies in aluminum foil before we went to sleep. The ghosts, he said, might be full of radium and could give us cancer if we didn't protect ourselves.

**24.** Seriously.

**25.** We quietly snickered, but not to his face.

**26.** Just before we were about to try to get some sleep—without the aluminum wrapping—Dad called us all back to the table, and he was glowing. Not from any radium, but from excitability. He'd had a call from Joe, who had a call from Tim, who had a call from the other Tim, who had a call from Bill, and blah, blah, blah, and, basically, the mayor wanted all of us to "take back our town." To do that, he instructed families to put every unsold scarecrow out around Crowville. He said the scarecrows did a good job at scaring the deer away from his vegetable garden, so he reasoned they'd keep ghosts away, too.

**27.** While the rest of us snacked on chocolate chip cookies and drank warm milk at the same table from which we hadn't moved, Dad darted into the garage and grabbed what had to be at least three dozen boxes of scarecrows. He was sweating so much that he didn't have to use a knife to cut the tape on the top of one of the boxes. His hand just went right through the cardboard.

**28.** He was also yelling about the hot glue gun and telling us to make sure it was warming up. Again, we were just chillin' at the table, snacking. He ran back into the garage and eventually got the glue going himself. He hung scarecrows on every door in the house. On the bathroom doors, he put one on each side. (Nearly a dozen ghosts flew by when he was on the toilet earlier in the day, and he was "traumatized.")

**29.** Once he had the station wagon loaded and was ready to go scaring the harmless ghosts away—for real, they would've annihilated the entire population in five seconds if they meant to do any harm—he came back inside and practically dragged us to the car. "Come on, team!" he shouted at us. "We can do this!" "We can scare those ol' ghosts back to where they came from!" "Woohoo!"

**30.** None of us, except him, had any interest in competitive sports or cooperative game play of any kind, so we laughed at his preppy enthusiasm. And just him in general. Again. But this time it was out loud and to his face.

**31.** When we pulled out onto the main drag, which in Crowville was, obviously, the only drag, we joined the caravan of others who were determined to scare the ghosts away. Most of the dads—and a few of the moms, I guess—were driving, and they had their windows rolled down, hooting and hollering to one another as the rest of us snickered. A brake light would appear abruptly, and we'd halt and have to wait for the dad or mom in front of us to get out and tie a scarecrow to a bush or a sign. Then, after we'd stopped for what seemed like a couple of hundred times within less than a mile, it was our turn—or Dad's. We refused, so he ran out by himself, after putting the car in park, and placed scarecrows anywhere he could think to put one. Mailboxes and doorsteps. The edge of cornfields. Empty dog houses. Beside a stray tabby cat. When he emptied one box, he ran back for another. Dad shook the scarecrows at the stuck-smiling ghosts and shouted. He was a personified version of the very thing he held in his hands. He waved his hands and jumped up and down all while shrilly howling. His voice was so high it sounded as if he'd sucked down a gallon of helium. (Adrenaline did some crazy things to that man.) Until all the scarecrows we possessed were lost amid the ghosts, he persisted.

**32.** Once he cleaned us out of scarecrows, he stepped on the brake and put us back into drive. The line of cars kept moving down the congested road because no one knew what to do next.

**33.** It has to be stated, for the record, that the ghosts were still out doing the same things they'd been doing since they'd arrived. You know, not hurting anyone and just floating around quietly.

**34.** As the night faded, Dad's energy did not. He went on and on about the ghosts and swore he wouldn't turn around. He wouldn't allow us to live in a place like Crowville anymore. It wasn't safe. It wasn't a good place to raise a family. He really didn't turn around either. All night he drove. He didn't stop until the sun rose and he was in Arkansas.

**35.** Or at least that's the story he told Mom on the phone at some point.

**36.** On Great Descension night, just as we were about to cross out of Crowville, Mom told my brother and me to jump out on her count to three, so after she rattled off a quick "one" and "two," we high-tailed it out of the old station wagon and went rolling down the sidewalk. After we brushed ourselves off, we walked back home.

**37.** We were the first ones to abandon the caravan, but we weren't the only ones. A few other people jumped out after seeing us. They walked back, shaking their heads and giggling, to their houses, too.

**38.** It was good to know that not everybody was scared of ghosts.

**39.** When I got in my bed, a handful of ghosts flew overhead. I tried to get their attention, but no matter how loudly I yelled or politely I asked, nothing worked. They kept on keeping on, oblivious to us and to the world. As more and more came in—and just as quickly left—my room, their novelty wore off, and my thoughts turned to the scarecrows. I realized that while they were fine, there was something they would never be able to keep away: fear. Fear. Fear. Fear. And on the day of the Great Descension, fear is what was really everywhere. No matter how many scarecrows anyone put out, that fear wasn't leaving.

**40.** But, you know, the longer I thought that night, I realized something. I was wrong. Fear did leave. It left when the last car turned right on the open highway out of Crowville. At that, I fell asleep smiling.

# THE
# MOONEATERS

**T**HEY, MOTHER AND SON, DREAMT it would end under a tree. The pair nestled in the darkness, clinging to the belief that one could—no would—take the other when the time came. She had promised him. He had promised her. Both had remained true so far. They were determined to keep something, and their word was now the only thing left.

***

The mother and son's tiny house stood deep inside what they knew only as "the woods." Their small construction, if you could really call it such, was fine for them and had been since the day they'd run from the open world and taken refuge inside it. The walls were sturdy, and the floor kept most cold drafts outside. Two windows, one facing the east and the other looking west, were broken, but old pieces of tape kept what needed to stay away outside. The roof, even with its splintered cracks, only let in a few snowflakes. The candles they burned rested on the floor, and the flames never grew strong enough to grow light past a couple of feet. The darkness is what kept them safe. Light was dangerous. What needed to stay out did. Or, at least, it had.

Inside, the boy sat on the dusty oak floor and colored the torn pages from an old coloring book. Birds, his mother had told him from before he could even remember. He'd never seen animals, but his mother told him that he would. The coloring, she thought, would help him not be scared when the time came.

"Am I the only kid?" the boy asked, looking up at his mother.

"You are," she assured him, cradling his cheeks with her hands.

"Are you the only mommy?"

"I am," she replied, squeezing his face before turning away to cough into her handkerchief.

When she looked down, she saw it was still there. She had hoped it was only a fluke the day before. A glitch with her eyes the week earlier. A brief slide into madness. A dream. A nightmare. She couldn't remember when it had begun. Why did it matter? There was no arguing its arrival.

The brightness of what had come from inside her was unusual. In a world where darkness provided protection, the shining, glowing tint seemed out of place. She had remembered her own mother's end, and this, she remembered, was how it had begun. Like mother, like daughter.

"Mommy, are you sick?" the boy asked.

"I'm fine. It's just a little cough. Pay attention to your coloring."

The boy ignored his mother's instructions. Although she had raised him, he still held a part of someone else inside him. Still innocent, but she could see his stubbornness growing. He put down his crayon and stood, glaring at his mother's ear.

She looked up at her son, watching his eyes, as they scanned the side of her face.

"You have something on you," he said, reaching out his hand.

The mother caressed the side of her face with her hand, slowly brushing up and down.

"It's nothing, son." She tucked her stray hairs behind her ear.

The boy, again, paid no attention to his mother. He reached down and hesitantly touched her face. It was the first time he'd touched her this way. She could feel his fear, and she scooted away from him.

"Mommy, you have something on you," he said, reaching toward her now with more confidence.

He bent and grabbed the unusual growth from the side of his mother's face and began to investigate it. "It's soft, Mommy," he said. "Like your hair."

The boy's touch evolved into a slow stroking movement. He bit his lip curiously as he felt of his mother's newfound strangeness. His world wasn't one that was familiar with softness.

Suddenly, as if struck with the epiphany that the object did not belong on his mother's face, he pulled on the growth. It didn't budge, but he kept pulling—yanking, tugging.

"Stop! Stop!" she cried.

"It's stuck to you, Mommy," he said. "I have to get it!"

"Please!" she pleaded.

She cried louder, but the boy didn't stop.

He gripped what grew on his mother's face again, and he pulled with all of his might, heaving and grunting. Sweat ran down her clenched face. The wetness caused the boy to refocus his grip. His tiny hands fumbling near her ear.

The mother sobbed. Her lips, pressed firmly together, trembled. Was it the pain? Was it the fear of already knowing?

Finally, it broke free, and the boy and mother watched it float to the ground.

The object rested on the cold floor. The boy stood over it, questioning what it could be. The coloring was unusual. Matte. Nearly opaque. But somehow reminiscent of the candle's struggling flame. The shape odder than anything he could recall ever seeing. Then, it struck him.

"Mommy, is that a leaf?" he asked.

She shook her head. "No," she said quietly. "It's a feather."

His eyes showed he understood. The mother opened her mouth to remind him to not be scared, but just as the first word hit the tip of her lips, a light appeared at their hidden house's door.

"The mooneaters," she whispered, clutching her son by his arm.

For him, there was no before. The boy had never lived in a world free of the mooneaters. The stories his mother told him haunted his dreams. In those stories, she couldn't remember the year or the season, and she couldn't quite recall how they began. She only knew that they were.

She recounted how the mooneaters, shoulder-on-shoulder, climbed on top of one another, reaching high enough to pull away the stars. Together, these trees of mooneaters swayed like fractured limbs battling the wind. Trees top heavy and certain to crash to the ground. She described the mooneaters with their long, dirty, bony fingers. Their disgusting hands extending into the sky and pinching the stars out of place. Feverishly and ferociously, growling and howling, they ate them. Night after night, they, these mooneaters, ate the stars. Their bellies glowed. They would fight one another to stand at the summit of each pile, where one of them would grab a star from the dying sky and toss it below. The tall group of beings would collapse, chasing after the helpless star. After it was gulped away, the towers would re-form, with greedy hands and reckless feet trying to make their way to the top once again. The madness would soon recommence, as another star was flung below.

After some time, and after all of the stars, and, yes, the moon, which was the last to go, were gone, the mooneaters were the only light left except for the stray ember or candle flame. They were full, but not content—of course. Not them. They began eating one another. Addicted to the glow the other bodies carried.

People were quick to join the mooneaters. People needed light. They said they couldn't live without it. Their crops would die. Their animals would be next. What about their kids? *I have to be a mooneater to save my family*, they reasoned. That's how the conversion began. Justifiable reasoning.

People who hadn't even participated in the destruction of the stars and moon wanted the glow. They, just like the ones already in possession of luminescent bodies, ripped into the others. They were all the same. Even if it took a few extra days or weeks, they were mooneaters.

The mooneaters became so eager for any resemblance of a glow that they chased down those who didn't have a trace of the moon or a star in their bellies. The whites of the eyes were enough.

The mother told her son how she'd watched boys his age abandon their own mothers to join the mooneaters. One boy—in a moment she would never forget—kicked his mother in the chin because she was trying to hold him back from joining the mooneaters. His leg packed so much power that the mother lost her grip. The boy, who couldn't have been older than ten, took off running toward a group of them. With a knife, he sliced open one of their bellies and removed a star. Just as he put it to his lips, another one ripped the boy apart, placing the star into an already lit body.

In her story, the mother didn't tell the boy everything. She didn't want him to know how the other mother, broken with loss or, perhaps, hungry for her own glow, walked into the circle of them and met the same fate as the little boy.

In the darkness, the mother blamed the mooneaters.

The mooneaters were the reason she couldn't go outside with her son.

The mooneaters were the selfish ones who killed all the animals.

The mooneaters were why everyone the mother had ever loved was gone.

The mooneaters were...

The mother and son stood motionless. The feather was before them, and it twitched softly against the floorboards. The candle flame cast a small, billowy shadow, which neared the wall. Neither person paid the unusual object any attention. Not with the mooneaters being present. The mother's hand slid carefully and quietly down her son's arm, as her grip loosened. She wanted his hand, and she moved until she grasped it.

The boy had held his mother's hands every day of his life. He knew its crevices. He recognized its calluses. What he felt was different now. Her hands were prickly—ticklish.

His eyes glanced to the place where their hands met, and he saw the blurry edges of the budding fibers under the shadows.

More feathers. They were covering her hands.

She coughed again.

He closed his eyes and held firmly.

She knew the woods. After all these years, she still could place every tree and every stream. She had told herself she couldn't forget them. If the mooneaters ever came, she would have to remember. And here they were.

The mother and son watched the brightness build around them. At first the light was only near the entrance. The gleaming bodies shone through even the smallest of cracks between the wooden door and the floor. Even along the walls, the previously unknown fractured lines in the paneling became clear.

The boy, unacquainted with such brightness, closed his eyes and turned his head to the still dark corner behind him. The light caused his eyes to tear.

"It's okay," the mother whispered as softly as she could, mistakenly believing her son was crying from fear.

The boy couldn't understand what she was saying, but he knew her words were kind.

The light's intensity continued to grow from the outside.

The mother remembered before the mooneaters, back when she would sit on the grass and look up at the sky. Her favorite memories were from when the moon shone so brightly that none of the stars could be seen. The moon, so seemingly alone, managed to be beautiful and strong.

The door that stood before her reminded her of those nights.

Rather than increasing the fear, the mounting brightness made the mother feel more focused—more aware of what she had to do.

"Blow out the candle," she said, her voice absent of even the faintest trace of quietness.

Without hesitating, he bent down and blew just as the door came down.

Her own mother's sickness had appeared suddenly. A doctor couldn't have helped. She'd simply reached her end.

She'd resisted the mooneaters. She, like her daughter, was one of the pure. When the coughing came with the splattering of blood and the feathers sprouting on her cracked, dry skin, she cried.

Her tears fell not because she was scared, which she was not. They dampened her cheeks because she knew it was finally over.

She could bask in the light once again.

She could roam the forests without a care.

She could fly away to a land absent of the mooneaters.

Just as the last feather sprang from the only unopened pore on her skin, she rose from her bed transformed. Changed into something new—something better, something free.

A mooneater broke into her bedroom and stood still, observing the unusual creature that flew around the room. This wasn't what the mooneater had expected to find.

The bird's white feathers beat the air rapidly and spun, looking as if it—she—were a shooting star. The mooneater salivated and patted its hands. It shook with glee.

The bird flew around the room, singing loudly and beautifully. The melody carried out of the small house and up into the nearby woods. Snow that had clung to the branches fell to the ground. The bubbling water in the nearby streams went quiet.

Then, the bird burst through the window and out into the open.

The mooneater ran toward the shattered glass, maniacally flailing its arms. But there was no use.

The bird was free.

The mother and her son had heard the mooneaters break down the door, and they could hear the dirty feet rumbling against the hard oak. The mother yanked at her son's arm. "Come. Come," she whispered. "We have to leave now. They'll rip us apart."

She coughed and spit onto the floor. "Remember our promise," she said.

The boy said, "I remember," and flecks of her phlegm ricocheted back to his arm.

In the darkness, he looked for his mother's eyes. *This must be what it's like to be a mooneater,* he thought. *To search and search for that whiteness—for that light.*

He stood still and stared in the direction from which her words had come. The boy could hear her. He could feel her hands pulling at his skin. He wanted to see her.

Her coughing continued. Now, worse than before.

She struggled to find air. Her breaths came rapidly and she fought and fought against herself until all that was left was a soft gurgle.

Then, just as she went quiet, the boy's wish was granted. He could see his mother—his transformed mother.

One of the mooneaters stood before him, glowing like what he imagined the moon must've looked like.

Oh, how the stories of the old nighttime sky had thrilled him.

The stars.

The constellations.

Of course, the moon.

But those small pleasures were gone from the boy's world, and it was the mooneaters who had taken them.

The mother, covered in majestic white plumes, twirled in the air.

The boy watched in awe.

She whistled and chirped loudly, calling her son to follow her, and he did. *Their promise. Their promise.*

As she dove over one mooneater and tumbled below another, the boy did the same. The giant claws tore at his skin, and their fists pounded into his young body. Their glowing, rotund bellies swayed in the place he had always known as home.

But the boy refused them. They would not eat him. They would not claim him.

His feet never stopped moving. Not even after they hit the grass.

He ran after his mother as she led him deep into the dark forest.

---

They, mother and son, dreamt it would end under a tree. The pair nestled in the darkness, clinging to the belief that one could—no would—take the other when the time came. She had promised him. He had promised her. Both had remained true so far. They were determined to keep something, and their word was now the only thing left.

The howls came from behind them. The mooneaters would never stop.

The boy didn't have any feathers. Not yet.

So, she did what any loving mother would do. She dove into him and knocked him onto the cold ground. Her sharp beak plunged into his skin. She flew up to the lowest branch and rested. Then, she flew into him again. Again. Again. Again.

All this time, he didn't make a sound. The feathers were coming.

The mooneaters would be too late.

# COMMENCEMENT

I

**T'S UNUSUALLY QUIET AS WE** gather in the cafeteria. We tell ourselves it's because our families are with us and we don't want to embarrass them, but deep down, we know the real reason.

Although our parents mingle, we don't. Instead, we locate our marked tables and sit down.

When we look around, we find each other in places that are unfamiliar. Steve Lamb, our quarterback, shrinks in a corner. It's the one that houses the pair of milk-stained trash cans—the same corner where the overhead fluorescent bulbs constantly seize. Steve's beside Marsha Lee, our worst majorette. She, at least, looks at home.

The lunchroom's lights blink twice, and Mr. Gabriel, our principal, enters from the unlit hallway. His shoes stick to the newly waxed floor as he trudges to the front of the packed room in his commencement robe. Our parents quietly duck away from their conversations and join us for the official start of the night they've spoken of for so long.

Mr. Gabriel smiles and waves. Then he clears his throat. "Welcome, welcome," he says, holding up his arms and waiting for the hum of silence to take over the cafeteria.

When it comes, he begins again. "While it's been difficult to see such fine young men and women leave at the beginning of summer for the past twelve years, it's an especially emotional graduation tonight. You all are our first class to make it all the way from kindergarten at our little academy. The way we've watched you all grow up—you kids seem just about like our own. With the education and love you've received from us, I know you all will have bright futures full of success and happiness. Things won't be the same after your graduation, but for now, before we know who among you is the valedictorian, enjoy your last meal together. Your teachers and I have worked all day to make it perfect for you, so teachers, come on in, and let's celebrate these graduates."

Our teachers, wearing robes themselves, file in behind our principal. Once they are all in the cafeteria, Mr. Gabriel yells, "Follow me!"

In a straight line, the teachers do as they are told as they circle out and then march back in again through the adjacent wall's set of double doors, still following their leader.

As they reenter, they have food. And lots of it.

Thanks to our parents' insistence, most of us haven't eaten today. Our eyes are locked on the location of the various foods. We can't help but notice when Mr. Gabriel, who has one of his arms wrapped around a metal bowl that is as round as he is, pulls out a golden handsaw from under his robe. "I'm always getting ahead of myself," he jokes at the edge of the first table where Alice Adams, our unopposed class president, sits with her family.

Once he recovers, he produces a pair of tongs instead. "Much better," he says.

Alice and her father howl laughing and hold out their perfectly white plates.

Mr. Gabriel guides his utensil into his bowl, bringing back a helping of chopped lettuce, carrots, and radishes. He repeats the process as he works his way around the room.

Ms. Lane, our biology teacher who is usually so kind and happy, can barely manage a smile as she follows behind Mr. Gabriel. She offers each of us a choice of salad dressing.

Our art teacher, Mr. Demings, is everyone's favorite, but he won't make eye contact as he passes us. His hands shake as he gives us our napkins. We ask him if he's okay, and he nods.

When our robotics teacher, Mr. Seth, closes out the parade with a tray carrying bowls of gold-flecked pomegranate and chocolate ice cream, our parents make jokes about our grades, searching for a nod, a smile, a laugh—

anything that might give a hint about who it will be tonight. Although he carries all the answers, he offers none.

None of our teachers do. Not Ms. Smith, Mr. Leon, Ms. Appleton, Mrs. Kim, Mrs. Sheryl, or even Coach Boyton.

We almost don't recognize them. For this, we try to not make them feel bad.

After all, they are the ones who have to help with what happens later.

A bell announces the end of the meal, and we are glad when the sound finally comes. The food has been gone for nearly half an hour for most of us.

Since they helped with the initial planning of everything, our parents know the rules.

They stand and begin their goodbyes.

No matter what happens, they are grateful we are theirs.

They are proud of us.

They are proud of us.

They are proud of us.

When they tell us they love us, at last, they look past our eyes and into a space we aren't sure we fully know.

We get one final embrace, and it lingers.

Then they leave and make their way to their reserved seats on the football field.

Mr. Gabriel goes back to the front of the cafeteria and asks us to line up as we did in rehearsals. The teachers split into two rows, and we find our places behind them in alphabetical order.

Poor Isaac Taylor. Thick glasses and dirty shoes. The ends of his pants look chewed. He can't remember where he's supposed to stand and keeps moving in and out of line. We know it won't be him.

We sometimes talk about Isaac's situation when he's not around. We wonder why his family doesn't send him to public school—why they pay for an education when they can't even afford clothes. The only answer we come up with is that they believe that by going here he has a *chance* at something more. He doesn't. But maybe they believe so.

Freckle-faced Terri Gillie is just about as lost as Isaac, but she figures it out, singing aloud as she asks us our last names. It won't be her either.

There are others, too, who we don't expect to be the one called tonight. Zane Carlisle. Sally Combs. Elijah Faust. Cheryl Tanner. Winston Wells. In class, we hated when they were asked to read. Most of us believe they couldn't—can't.

"Is everyone in place?" Mr. Gabriel asks, not expecting—or waiting for—an answer. "Let's take our final hallway walk together. Think of all the memories you made here. Think of your teachers. Of your friends."

We begin our final tour as soon as the last word leaves his lips.

As we pass by the open doors that house our empty desks, some of us cry. Some of us laugh. Some of us walk quietly with the pleasant company of ourselves.

We remember books we read and equations we solved. We think of conversations we wished we'd had and arguments we should've given up.

We pass posters we designed, words we penned, and baseboards we scuffed.

We remember, and we mourn.

Mr. Gabriel halts our memory march before we get to the door that opens outside to the football field, the door beside the wall that houses all the official valedictorian portraits. "Remember, kids, it's an honor to be the valedictorian. No other school in the world gives its top student the gift that we do."

We nod and hang our heads.

All of us except Isaac Taylor. He, for the millionth time, asks Mr. Gabriel to explain how being valedictorian is an honor.

Mr. Demings steps out of line and puts his hand softly against Isaac's back. "Don't you worry about it, buddy," he whispers. "I don't think it'll be you."

"Okay."

Mr. Demings smiles and squeezes the boy's shoulder.

Mr. Gabriel goes to Mr. Demings and says something we can't completely make out, but the end of the conversation is loud enough for all of us to catch. "It's wrong is what it is," Mr. Demings says.

"But not wrong enough for you to leave?"

"Alright now," Mr. Gabriel says, turning to us again. "The music will begin any second, and when it does, walk to your seat just as we practiced. Slowly. Keep the same pace as me and your teachers. Your parents have paid a lot of money for your education—and your opportunity, and I'm sure they want pictures of you on your special night."

We stand in silence for only a handful of seconds before the music kicks on. "Let's go! Let's go!" Mr. Gabriel says, waving his arms above his head and motioning forward with his whole body.

Before the stadium's lights burn through the overhanging shadow of the school we walk from, he turns around. "Good luck," he says. And he means it.

We march to our chairs and watch as our classmates go to theirs. Valerie Williams and Thomas Zaniski nearly run across the manicured field as they try to escape the gaze of the ready-to-be-seated audience. When Valerie and Thomas get to their respective destinations, they sit down and quickly stand again, realizing their mistake. Then, like the rest of us, they look around and smirk awkwardly, waiting for the music to stop.

When the speakers slowly begin to fade, Alice Adams goes to the podium and asks us to continue standing as she leads us through the pledge and a prayer.

The way she goes about it is pure Alice. It's not at all surprising when we realize we still have our hands over our hearts by the time she lets out a breathless "amen."

She doesn't move to her seat, though; instead, without any kind of warning, she starts singing. She's halfway through before we even know what the song is. "Please join me in singing our alma mater!" she finally shouts.

Most of us don't. We never took the time to learn the words. But our parents sing. Loudly, bursting with pride for the school they made—and continue to make—possible.

We notice when Alice carries the closing note too long. It's the first time any of us feel like we see her as really being one of us. After all these years, it's now that we (almost) don't hate her.

She bows, and Mr. Gabriel approaches the podium. He fidgets with the microphone and taps its covering until the speakers squeal. "Testing, testing," he laughs, knowing already the sound system works perfectly fine.

"It is such a beautiful evening for a commencement. I'm honored to be standing before you as principal of this incredible institution, celebrating yet another tremendous class of young people. Kids, like I told you at the feast, it's been difficult these past few years to see such fine young men and women leave us, but I know each of you will have a bright future full of success and happiness. While I believe this to be true for every student who sits before me, I know it as *the* truth for one of you. We'll find out who takes the honor as class valedictorian soon enough, but for now, let's get you those diplomas."

A steady applause sweeps across the field.

Mr. Seth, who sits to the side of the stage away from the rest of the teachers, rises from his seat and brings two tall cardboard boxes to the square table beside the podium. Once the boxes are in place, he reaches under his robe and brings out a golden butcher knife that's as big as his forearm. He guides the blade along the taped crease of the first box's cardboard lid.

Mr. Gabriel nods at him. "Glad you got some extra use out of that thing," he says loud enough for the microphone to catch.

Mr. Seth chuckles and walks to the unlit edge of the field that houses the school's robotics workshop.

"Let's hear a round of applause for Mr. Seth. We couldn't do commencement without him," Mr. Gabriel says.

We follow suit. As Mr. Gabriel waits for us to settle, he reaches into the top box and retrieves the first diploma.

We look around at one another for a last glimpse. We know our parents believe what is to follow is an honor, but it doesn't seem that way to us. When we hold meetings about it after school, our parents tell us we don't understand— that we should be grateful for the education they've paid for us to have. More than that, they say, we should be appreciative of having the opportunity to be valedictorian. To be more than graduates—more than humans.

At the end of the day, we are their children. We listen. We nod. We owe it to them—to ourselves—to try our best. No matter what.

Mr. Gabriel's voice interrupts our gazes. "Graduates, please stand. As I call your name, approach the stage. Alice Adams."

Soft applause goes with Alice as she steps on the stage's platform and receives her diploma. When the camera flashes, she smiles so brightly that it looks like she's eaten a bucket of stars.

"Carlos Amos."

"Cheyenne Barnes."

"Zane Carlisle."

"Sally Combs."

"Donny Easton."

"Laney Easton."

Once Laney gets her first picture, Donny jumps back on stage. Donny, Laney, and Mr. Gabriel pose for a photo that that we know will decorate the Easton family's living room through eternity.

Mr. Gabriel continues with our names, reading each one perfectly as if he knows us as well as he knows himself.

"Elijah Faust."

"Terrie Gillie."

A cacophony of airhorns and screamers ring from the reserved seating section, and Mr. Gabriel huffs. We all hear him, but that doesn't stop the Gillies. They blow into their plastic toys until long after Terrie finds her way back to her seat. "T-er-rie! T-er-rie! T-er-rie!"

"Steve Lamb."

"Marsha Lee."

Mr. Gabriel tosses the first box behind the table and rips the tape off the next box. He rushes through a bunch of us.

"Isaac Taylor."

Another series of airhorns unsettle the air. Isaac goes up the exit side of the stage, forgets to stand in place for the photographer, and exits through the entrance.

"Valerie Williams."

Mr. Gabriel holds up one final diploma cover. "And our final graduate of the evening, Mr. Thomas Zaniski."

Thomas runs across the stage and then back to his seat. Six foot, eight inches tall. Math team captain. A humble version of Alice Adams—and scared of his shadow. We wonder what will become of him out in the real world.

The same song that played during our procession begins over the sound system. At the first note, each of us takes a long, deep breath.

Mr. Seth marches from the workshop, and he's not alone. He's followed by the twelve valedictorians since our school began.

Our parents stand and cheer.

It's obvious the Gillies and Taylors aren't the only ones with airhorns.

We are all seated except for Alice. She's jumping and squealing. Brandon Briarspeck, her ex-boyfriend, was last year's valedictorian, and she hasn't seen him since before he and his parents left for last year's commencement feast. He's first in line behind Mr. Seth. "Brandon! Brandon!" she cries, but he doesn't acknowledge her.

The closer he gets, the quieter Alice grows. She stops bouncing, and she sits back down. Whether it's his glowing eyes or his steel-tracked, wheeled feet that do her in, it's impossible to say. Carlos puts his hand on her shoulder and squeezes her gently. "Maybe it will be you tonight," he mouths.

Alice shakes her head. "I don't want it!" she says loudly. "I don't want it anymore!"

Seeing him in front of us, it's clear that Alice—finally—really speaks for all of us.

Mr. Seth marches to the edge of the commencement stage and lowers a ramp over the stairs.

The valedictorians roll up, one by one. Isaac Taylor, of all of us, jumps up and points, noticing it first. "Look at their legs! Their legs!"

Immediately, we see it, too. On all of them. Little flecks of cut, loose skin flap just below the hems of their golden robes, their own wheels working as imperfect scalpels.

We close our eyes, and we wait. It's all we can do now.

Their parents and grandparents blindly cheer just as proudly as they surely did on the valedictorians' own commencement nights.

Mr. Seth shakes Mr. Gabriel's hand once the past valedictorians are in place, and the two men stand behind the microphone.

"Friends," Mr. Gabriel says. "It's that time. It's no secret that we keep our students' grades hidden until commencement night. As we all know—and decided upon back in those not-so-long-ago foundational meetings—it's a pass or a fail through the years, and that's it. We keep the exact grades hidden away on a file maintained by myself and Mr. Seth. We want our valedictorians to have a normal existence until the moment they become something greater, which your generous financial contributions certainly allow. Tonight—now— we reveal the one who is the top of the class. That student will join the other valedictorians and live among them thanks to Mr. Seth and his Legacy Robotics Technology. Brain preserved. Heart removed. He or she will, in a way the rest of us will not, live forever. It's an incredible, beautiful, beautiful thing that you've all made possible."

An airhorn shoots through the breeze. "We love you, Terrie Gillie!"

Not to be outdone, another follows. "Good luck, Isaac Taylor!"

"T-er-rie! T-er-rie! T-er-rie!"

"I-I-saac! I-I-saac! I-I-saac!"

"T-er-rie! T-er-rie! T-er-rie!"

"I-I-saac! I-I-saac! I-I-saac!"

"T-er-rie! T-er-rie! T-er-rie!"

"I-I-saac! I-I-saac! I-I-saac!"

The battle continues until Mr. Gabriel finally interrupts. "Please," he says harshly. He clears his throat. "Please," he corrects himself, "hold your celebrations until the announcement."

Mr. Seth eyes Mr. Gabriel and bites his lip as he steps to the center of the podium.

"Brandon, come forward," Mr. Seth says into the microphone. Brandon does as he's told, rolling slowly to his place at the front. "Show us the heart."

Brandon unclasps his hands and unveils the tiny golden computer that will go into the new valedictorian's chest—our valedictorian's chest—and hands it off to Mr. Seth.

"Thank you," our robotics teacher says.

Our parents "ooh" and "aah," and Mr. Seth and Brandon wave to the crowd, indicating that their part is over.

"Wow," Mr. Gabriel says, reclaiming his spot at the microphone. "That is something. Thank you both. And thank you to all of our past valedictorians. It is an honor to be among you tonight."

Our bodies squirm in our seats, and we try not to look about. We know how it works. Our parents told us. Our teachers did. Our textbooks detailed the whole process. We know everything.

"Teachers, will you come to the front as I make this year's announcement?"

They do as they are told.

Most of us are crying.

*It's an honor*, we tell ourselves.

*It's what we've worked for*, we say.

*It's what our parents paid so much for.*

*It's an honor. It's an honor. It's an honor.*

Mr. Demings won't look up from the grass. He reaches out to Ms. Lane and squeezes her free hand. She brushes at her cheek with her other one.

Mr. Gabriel moves his lips so they are against the microphone's covering. "The honor of valedictorian goes to," he says, pausing and drumming his hands against the top of the podium. When he stops, he yells the name into the fragile silence: "Mr. Thomas Zaniski!"

Our teachers run toward us, circling Thomas' seat. Those of us around him leap out of the way.

"You've made your parents proud," we say.

"Congratulations," we tell him.

Thomas tries to escape, but there's no use. Coach Boyton grabs him by the legs and drags him away from his chair. Thomas reaches for it and then at all the others, but it's no use.

"It's an honor, Thomas," we mumble to him as he passes by. "It's an honor. It's an honor."

"No!" he yells to us. "I don't want it! No! No!"

"Being valedictorian is an honor," Coach Boyton assures him. "I hope my son gets it next year."

Thomas cries; he begs us to help him.

He flails about as he's carried away to the workshop.

The other valedictorians slowly roll off the stage behind Mr. Seth. They follow behind Thomas and our teachers.

"Congratulations, graduates," Mr. Gabriel says. "And goodnight."

He already has his golden handsaw out again before he's clear of the podium.

He runs to the reserved seats and gets Thomas' parents, who are glowing under the stadium's lights. The other parents are giving them high fives and patting them on their backs.

Mr. Gabriel pulls them away, and they rush to catch up with the others as they head deeper into the workshop's shadow.

Alice takes off her graduation cap, and we follow her lead. Her voice is barely detectable as she rattles off a quick "one," "two," and "three."

As we toss our hats into the air, all we can think about is facing our parents. We wonder if they really are still proud of us now that it's not their last name that will live on forever. We've tried so hard not to disappoint them.

# DOLLS
# FOR THE END
# OF THE WORLD

**T**HE WARMTH CAME AND LEFT, and, no sooner, it left and came. There was no way to guess what the world would become. At least it remained. Charred oak trees surrounded by misplaced puddles. Rivers as black as burnt cherries. Sputtering flames along the receding riverbanks. Days shorter and, still, longer.

Patrick stood on the cliff and looked down at where he'd come. In his arms, Theodore. Always Theodore. A boy and his doll. They were and they were not. Broken, but together. With a voice, yet voiceless.

Still searching—these two defenders of the future.

Patrick's father sat on the edge of his son's bed and stared into his hazel eyes. He refused to look elsewhere because then he would see them. The dolls stacked in Patrick's rocking chair. The dolls along the scratched dirty floor. The dolls hanging from the ceiling fan. The dolls, of course, scattered on the bed.

"Pa, can't I get a story tonight? For my birthday?" Patrick asked quietly, turning his face toward his pillow.

His father didn't hesitate. His hand flew as if he were a fox and his son's face the prey. Hungry. Vicious. "Ain't no story gonna make you a man," he said.

Patrick pulled his hand up and felt the warm sting of his cheeks. The mark would fade just as the others had.

His eyes remained downward. He searched, among the many, for his favorite and longest companion: Theodore, the doll with a drawn-on navy smile and black button eyes. "I'm sorry you had to see that, Theodore," he whispered.

His father snatched the doll from Patrick's hands and tossed it onto the floor. Theodore's stuffed body bounced with no thump or ding. The quiet was worse than the taunting. His father stood, and his foot found the doll. He smothered Patrick's beloved friend. "Yeah, Theodore. I'm so sorry you had to see that," he mocked.

Patrick sat up in his bed and made a fist. He shook it in the air surrounding his father's face. "Don't touch my doll. You'll hurt him."

"It's a doll."

"He's my friend."

"You don't have any friends."

"You're just mad because you are scared of what's coming."

"Oh," Patrick's father said. "Something's coming, huh? I bet Theodore told you that, too, didn't he?"

Patrick sat still, staring at his father. "That's why he and the others are here. He read about the signs in a book," he said.

"Ha! And don't ever say that I'm scared. I'm not scared of anything." Sweat trickled down the man's forehead.

"Yes you are. You know how I know?" Patrick asked, pointing to the window. "Because it's not just coming anymore. It's here."

He watched his father's reflection among the blazing background.

There are some things that can't be contained.

Shoes already covered Patrick's feet when he hit the ground. He lifted the mattress and grabbed his frayed satchel. Two pairs of jeans, three ragged shirts, a couple of unmatched socks, and a pair of dirty underwear. It was all the clothing he had.

He circled the room, grabbing his dolls and stuffing them into the bag with his clothes. All of them except Theodore, whom Patrick held in his arms.

"We have to go," the boy said to his father. "The house won't stand long."

But his father didn't budge. Shock held him in its trance.

"Pa," Patrick called as he touched his father's shoulder. "Pa, come on."

The man remained as still as an ancient stone, hiding his own mystery. Patrick looked at his father again, but he saw nothing more than an empty silhouette.

"Pa, Theodore says we need to go now."

Trees collapsed. Embers crackled. But the man at the window began to laugh. Uncontrollably. Hysterically. Shamelessly. "You're not special, boy. Don't make the mistake of thinking you are."

"What?" Patrick asked.

"Be a man. Come sit here and let's die together."

"Theodore says—"

"Forget it. You never were much of a son anyhow. Go on—go running with your dolls."

Patrick reached for his father's shoulder again, but his father intercepted the boy's touch and pushed him to the ground.

He regained his footing. Then, he turned to Theodore and asked, "Now is when I do it?"

He waited only a second before he reached behind his back and pulled out the first doll his fingers found. He placed it at his father's feet. Loneliness was too cruel of a thing for even him.

Patrick sprinted toward the house's front door.

As he turned the knob, an explosion came from his bedroom.

"Goodbye, Pa," Patrick said, and he ran.

Stars fell and died. Dirt floated and sparkled. Everything was nothing, but, still, there was something. Patrick, with Theodore and his sack full of dolls, played dodgeball against the crashing world. He didn't have a choice. He had to survive. Theodore told him as much.

Patrick's feet kept moving even as smoke choked him. He coughed and spat, but it did little good. Only more came.

He tasted metal. Or was it blood? It was better not to know.

The explosions kept them hidden for a while, but tears streaked his face upon the sound of the first one. The crying. The moans. The fear. The sounds came so often that they became a part of the settling breeze.

They brought the boy comfort because to not hear them meant death.

"I know. I know," Patrick said to Theodore. "I'm going."

Patrick chased the first voice until he found it. A man—much older than his father. Patrick fell to his knees and brushed away the dirt and leaves that clung to the man's body. He held him. Then, he hugged him.

"It's going to be okay," Patrick said. "I promise."

The man was quiet as he looked up at the boy's eyes.

"This is for you." Patrick said, grabbing a doll from his bag and handing it to the man.

The man wrapped his arms around it just as Patrick had done to the man. His shoulders fell as he breathed—smoother and softer.

"Do you hear the others crying?" Patrick asked.

"Yes," the man said.

"I have to help them."

So, he did.

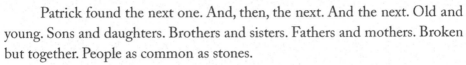

Patrick found the next one. And, then, the next. And the next. Old and young. Sons and daughters. Brothers and sisters. Fathers and mothers. Broken but together. People as common as stones.

Each took a doll from the boy.

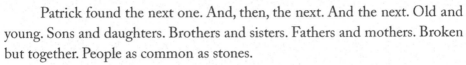

He cried when he found his father. Cradled in his charred arms was the doll Patrick had left at his feet.

Patrick sat down with Theodore by his side. "Do you think I'll ever be a man?" he asked. But Theodore didn't answer. And he never would again.

Patrick looked up and saw them. All of them he'd helped.

Clutching their dolls, they waited to hear what the boy would say.

# THE CREATOR

**W**HEN HE FOLDS ALONG THE lines, he is still. Before this moment, he hasn't felt at peace since before her eyes closed far too soon.

What he meticulously creates isn't really much of a figure yet—just the dream of one.

In this free class, open to anyone and inside the back room at the local craft supply store, he doesn't interrupt the instructor or ask unnecessary questions. He listens, and he folds. Each step like a ritual. More sacred than a promise—a secret.

The other students are here to indulge in a hobby. Not the man. He's here to be reminded of what it means to love.

His body, like a protective shield, crouches over the desk. His hands cover the completed paper creation. Slowly, he peeks between his fingers. As he does, he says a prayer. He asks that his lips will have the power to breathe life.

When the instructor comes by to check on the man's progress, she notices his desk is already clean except for the presence of his cupped hands. He nods. She thanks him for coming and goes on to the next student.

When the man opens his hands and sees how his paper creation waves, with surprisingly uncrooked arms, the man waves back and laughs. At his paper boy—his paper son.

The man gently tucks his paper son inside his shirt's pocket. The man doesn't button the flap, so it's easier for him to look down inside the cotton crevice to see his paper son as he leaves the store.

The rain catches the man by surprise when he steps outside. He runs to his truck and scrambles with his keys.

When the man reaches in his pocket, his paper son is gone—not *gone* gone, but gone enough. The perfect folds of the paper son are no more. His hands are no different from his head. He is translucent and ripped.

The man waves at the boy again, but his son stays limp.

The man scoops his son from the soaked corner of his wet shirt and holds him against the air conditioner. He doesn't come to. Not even when he's dry.

The man goes inside the store and asks the instructor if there is any way to repair the damage. She tells him there is not, but she reminds him that he now has the knowledge of how to create. She encourages him to try again.

The man thanks her and explores the shelves for supplies. He buys three different kinds of paper. He can make another son. Maybe a daughter.

When the man is back at home, he sits at his kitchen table. He takes out the paper and begins drawing lines. But he can't stay focused.

His hands shake. The paper tears and crumples. The man has no choice. He tosses the paper away.

A few raindrops patter on the roof, and the man thinks of his son. He will every time it rains.

# THE GALACTIC HEALERS

**F**ROM MY BEDROOM WINDOW, I watched them descend on our highest hilltop. Their spaceship looked like the setting sun—slow and sure, but the sun had a habit of fading. Their vessel did not. It still glowed in the evening sky as it sat perched above us all.

My heart danced in my chest.

My prayers had been heard.

I leapt from my desk and ran toward them.

"Healers! Healers!" I cried.

I didn't stop for shoes. Or even for a shirt. I sprinted out the front door.

My legs burned as I climbed the hill. Jagged rocks cut the soles of my bare feet. My breaths came quickly and with sharp pains. Still, though, I ran. I didn't stop until I stood at the spaceship's door.

—

"Healers!" I called, gasping. "It's Lian! I'm the one who prayed you here!"

The spaceship shook as the engine died. The door lowered with a soft rumble. Out they stepped. A dozen slender, soaring bodies with translucent skin stepped onto the earth's scorched floor. The same brains. The same lungs. They, too, had hearts pumping blood throughout their bodies.

I moved to welcome them, but a hand grabbed my shoulder and threw me onto the ground.

"Go home," my father said. "Go home now." His voice was quiet, but angry. He didn't blink as he looked down at me.

"It's because of me that they're here," I explained. "I prayed them here." I planted my hands on the ground and sprang back to life, brushing off the dirt that clung to my body.

"You are a child, Lian. You don't know anything."

My father stepped toward me, but another foot moved at the same time. My father paused. We both looked up and saw one of the healers. It extended an arm and pointed at me—at the bright crimson trail that began at my ear and ran down my neck. The healer took another step toward me, but my father stepped between us.

"Don't!" my father commanded at the healer. "Don't lay a finger on my boy. He's sick."

The other remaining adults appeared behind my father. Stoically, they stood. Some flexed their arms. Others cracked their knuckles.

They didn't last a night before they demanded to go inside the spaceship. I followed them.

Inside, the largest healer cocked its head toward me. Its eyes questioning, but kind.

"It will be okay," I said, reassuringly.

It looked away and turned its attention to the adults, who explored the blooming landscape along the spaceship's vibrant floor.

Greens and yellows filled the spaceship. Water flowed along the strange vessel's walls. Birds floated from one blossoming flower to another. Giant plum blooms swayed among the flutter of the various creatures' wings.

"It's like in the books," I said to my father.

"Hush, Lian!" he said.

"Why do you beasts have such extravagances? Did you take them from us? Is that why our earth is dying?"

The healers remained silent, looking from themselves to the adults.

"They are here to help us," I said from the corner of the ship. "They are our saviors."

The adults grunted. A few chuckled.

"Help us what?" my father asked.

"Help us get well," I replied.

As soon as I said it, I felt the familiar feeling return. I touched my ears and looked down at my hands. The blood covered my fingers.

My father grabbed my soaked hands, and he rubbed them until the blood covered him just the same.

"Does it look like you are well?" He grabbed my neck and turned it so that I was forced to see the blood running down my neck and onto my chest. "Does it?" he yelled. "These aliens are thieves. Murderers. They are here to finish us off. Why can't you understand that?"

I bit my lip and stared at him. Tears rolled down my face.

"Go home, Lian," he said.

So, I turned toward the exit and walked.

A healer stood at the door with one of the purple flowers that sprouted from the spaceship's floor and broke it in half. The gooey insides dripped from the stem, but the healer cupped the remains into its hands.

The healer looked at my father and held out its palm. "It's okay," I said.

My father remained still, willing to see proof of the miracle I touted.

The healer moved to the ground and pulled me beside it. It crossed its legs and brought me into its hold. It slathered the flower's juice on my ear.

My body quivered at the surprising coolness of its hands—and of the tingling that came from the sap.

There were no mirrors in the spaceship, but there didn't have to be for me to know that the bleeding had stopped.

———

My father ran to me, and, for the first time in years, he held me. "Your ears!" he cried. "You're not bleeding!" He turned to the adults. "He's not bleeding!" he repeated. Tears dampened his cheeks as he cried inside the healers' spaceship.

He grabbed his sleeve and wiped his face. "Give me the flowers," he mumbled. But his voice soon found its footing. "Give me the flowers," he said. "Give me all of the flowers!"

The healers looked at him, unaware of the meaning of his words.

He pointed to the flowers and then to himself. Quickly. Angrily. He repeated his motions.

The healers chirped and twirled circular movements to one another. Then, they nodded.

They bent toward the floor and plucked all of the blooming flowers on their spaceship and handed them to my father.

He stuffed them into his pockets so tightly that some of the stems burst open. The medicine ran down his legs and onto the floor. Wasted forever. Gone.

"I have to protect him," he said. "My boy is the only child left."

He went to the door, and he led us back to our home.

———

I prayed all night. That they wouldn't give up on us. That they would stay. That they would help us. That we would be okay.

———

I found them outside the next morning. They were working in the ashy dirt that used to be our harvesting field.

They saw me watching them from behind the glass, so they signaled me over.

They pointed to the ground and began their precise movements. Their long fingers dug deep into the dry earth—so deep that the dirt became damp—and they made long, thick rows.

One healer grabbed my hand and placed a seed from the spaceship on my open palm. Carefully, it moved my hand into the dirt and turned it over. The healer led me to cover the seed. It cupped my hands and, together, we tightly packed the dirt surrounding the unborn life.

"Is this how we make the medicine?" I asked. "The flowers?"

The healer only smiled. I pointed to my ears. It nodded and pointed to where we had buried the seed.

I held out my hand and told the healer to wait. "Water," I said, enunciating the word. "I'll bring some water for the seed."

The healer watched me leave. I turned back and waved, but the healer didn't understand.

When I returned from our only remaining stream, the adults were standing in the field, watching the healers.

My father was the one who saw the cup in my hand.

He ran toward me and slapped it from my grip. The container and the water it held collapsed below us, falling onto the cracked earth.

"We don't give our water away, Lian. Especially not to them."

"It's for the seeds. To help them grow," I explained.

"To help the seeds grow? You see a flower on a spaceship and think that now we can grow whatever we please in this dead dirt? It doesn't work that way."

"The healers are here to help us. They are showing us how to rebuild."

"Healers? Is that what you call them? They are aliens. They crashed, and we got lucky that we found their spaceship before they could leave. Did you see them offering any flowers to us before we went on their ship? No, we had to take them."

"They are healers. I prayed for them to come. You barely gave them time to get off the ship before you—"

"You are a kid," he interrupted. "You don't know anything about praying. You don't know anything about living. You sure don't know anything about dying. You don't even understand that that's what's happening to you. You are dying, Lian. You've got the sickness. We'll all have it soon. Pray all you want, but there is nothing that can save us."

I couldn't speak anymore—not to the person who stood in front of me. I took my fist and, with every bit of strength that remained in me, I punched him in the chest.

I watched him collapse on the ground, coughing and spitting, and I ran to the healers. I leapt into the arms of the first one I came to, and I begged it to take me with it.

It cradled me against its body.

The only thing the healers were guilty of was loving me.

I should've known better. Love left our world a long time ago.

The healers tried to explain why they had held me, but no one could understand. They clicked their tongues and stretched their lips across their broken, jagged teeth. The words they searched for remained out of reach. All that came out were squeals and hisses.

Their towering bodies shook as they tried to explain themselves.

I told the adults that it was my fault. I was the one who pushed my father down. I was the one who ran to them.

They wouldn't listen. They never did.

There was nothing left for me to do, so I sat on the ground and wept.

The wind swirled viciously against my bare arms. Rocks rolled past me.

The earth shook when the healers finally took off. My whole body shuddered, and, for a moment, I thought that I still might go with them.

I imagined a long arm reaching from the sky, plucking me from my hell.

I prayed that they could somehow still save me.

Dead leaves and rocks flew into my face, but I didn't flinch. I owed the healers that much. I sat still and watched the orange sky as the healers' bright and metallic sphere smoldered up into the atmosphere until it was no more.

A ringing in my ears began as soon as they were out of sight. The blood wasn't far behind.

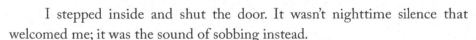

I stayed on the hill until nightfall, sitting in a puddle of my own blood.

I talked to the healers although they couldn't hear me.

I prayed again. Maybe the healers would come back in the morning. Maybe they would give us one more chance.

I tried to remember the people who once lived. Their laughs too far gone to be heard. Their smiles broken in my imagination. Life must've been a beautiful thing once.

When I realized the sky held no more miracles for me, I walked home.

It would be a fine place to die.

I stepped inside and shut the door. It wasn't nighttime silence that welcomed me; it was the sound of sobbing instead.

My father cowered in the corner. His veins bulged under his skin. His bloody hands clung to his ears. He pushed into his skull as hard as he could. The pressure didn't work for the others. I knew that it wouldn't work for him either.

But the flowers. The flowers might save him.

I ran to the bowl where he kept the items that occupied his pockets.

Then, I saw them. Brown and stiff. Dead. Broken. Lost forever.

There was a steady wailing rising from beyond the window. The other adults. The sickness had come for them all.

I kneeled beside my father and cradled his head against my shoulder.

I sat with him for the rest of the night—until a light began to flicker at the horizon.

The sun? The healers?

I closed my eyes, and I prayed.

# RESTORED

**F**OR TWO HOURS, MY BROTHER Marcus has been plotting his theft at Ms. Simone's Cleansing Fountain. Rather than hurrying to get it over with, we cower behind a leaning, old, rusty tower. He peeks his head around the corner and looks back at me. He repeats his movement over-and-over again. I sit and wait.

"Just imagine, Ben. Mother back to her old ways. She'll forget about Danny getting sick and will be laughing and playing with us again in no time," he says.

Without taking much of a breath, he continues his justification. "Ms. Simone produces enough tears for everyone in the whole village. Think about it. That's maybe, what? Thousands of gallons of tears? That woman does nothing but cry. What is taking a little extra going to do? Nothing, I say. Absolutely nothing."

I look at Marcus and shrug.

"Nothing," he insists again as he finally stands and heads toward her. I jump to my feet and follow him.

"I thank you for your tears. My family will not forget your sacrifice," a man says to Ms. Simone. His family nods in agreement and walks away.

"Your pain," an elderly woman says as her voice fades into mumbles.

"Thank you for your love," says a mother.

"Thank you. Thank you. Thank you," voices echo.

A calm crowd surrounds the base of the Cleansing Fountain; the visitors stand in awe of Ms. Simone. She sits in the center and rocks and cries. Her sobs are loud. Her face glows with a burnt redness, as if blood could burst from her wrinkled pores at any second.

A member of each family takes a single vial and fills it. Most drink what she sheds while there, thank her, and then walk away with a revered silence. Others quickly swallow the vial's contents without even a glance at Ms. Simone. Even the few who do not show appreciation take that which she gives.

Marcus approaches the Cleansing Fountain's waters and fills a vial. "Thank you, Ms. Simone. Your tears helped my family before, and they will again," he says, telling his tainted version of the truth.

I stand back and listen to Marcus. His voice is stern with apparent sincerity. He stares at the old woman who weeps for us all.

———

"Marcus," I say to my brother. "How are you going to get Mom to drink Ms. Simone's tears? We've already had our dose for the—"

"Look, Ben," Marcus says, cutting me off. "Let me worry about this, okay? And I don't care if she's had her annual fill or not. It obviously didn't work."

"But what if it makes her sick? More than she already is?" I ask.

He doesn't acknowledge me, so I turn from my brother and walk away.

———

"Ben, Mother, dinner is ready," Marcus says from the kitchen.

I enter the room first and grab my plate. "This is yours," Marcus says. "Take it and sit down."

I don't argue; instead, I take what he gives me, and I sit at the table. Mom enters and takes her food and drink in silence. We sit and eat.

When she finishes with her food, she reaches for her milk. Marcus smiles at me and winks.

But I can't let her do it.

Just before her hand can grasp it, I reach to give her my glass. She takes it as I take hers, and I chug the milk full of tears.

Before Marcus has a chance to do anything, the floors begin to shake. The crackling, wooden panels roll in waves. Then, from far away, a delicate humming sound approaches our house. The softness is no more. Our windows shatter. The walls pulsate.

Mom grabs Marcus by the arm and pulls him under the table.

I pause long enough to look at her, the way she holds him. It's now that I know that Mom was never really gone from us. What she was experiencing was something else—something the people in our village try to wash away.

I stand from the table to face the kitchen's window.

"Ben, get away from there! Come here!" Mom shouts to me.

"Ben!" shouts Marcus.

I ignore them both. Through the broken glass, I peek above the hill and watch the newly-glowing water, Ms. Simone's tears, flowing, now, upward into the clouds. The sound of cries washes over me. Yelling echoes throughout our village.

"You shouldn't have taken the extra vial," I say to Marcus as I reach for the doorknob.

I don't wait for him to reply as I take off running to the scene of my brother's crime.

Ms. Simone no longer cries, and her chair no longer rocks.

Instead, she is face down in her pool of tears.

Surges of the remnants of her tears still shoot into the sky, but what is left of her work is nearly gone.

The crowds that earlier thanked her are no longer as kind; no one tries to pull her out of the Cleansing Fountain. Men and women, young and old—they all push her body out of the way so they can gather what remains as the Fountain's water sprinkles off of the ascending stream.

"I need my fill for next year. Please!" an old man shouts.

"What about me! I need this. I have a sick father. I can't bear it if he dies. I beg you!" a young woman cries.

Panic overwhelms the entire lost village.

At the Fountain, there are fights for tears. Down the hill, others run with buckets toward the place where Ms. Simone rocked.

My eyes are already growing heavy, and I realize what I have to do. For Mom and Marcus. For all of the other names and faces I know.

I walk to the center of the Cleansing Fountain and fix my chair.

Once the first tear falls, I can't stop.

# A COMPLICATED CORRESPONDENCE

From: Wiley Rougy
Sent: Thursday, March 26, 2020 3:02 PM
To: Maverick Hamline <yomomluvsme@theeservice.com>;
<rebelluvshismom@electronicstorks.com>
Subject: My FRIGGIN Dad!

he murdered my FRIGGIN phone, bruhs!! hit me up on here. i'm like a dad now or whatever.

From: Maverick Hamline
Sent: Thursday, March 26, 2020 3:45 PM
To: Wiley Rougy <yafavboi@onlinedelivery.com>;
<rebelluvshismom@electronicstorks.com>
Subject: RE: My FRIGGIN Dad!

dude. u emailin now? and congrats i guess?

From: Wiley Rougy
Sent: Thursday, March 26, 2020 3:45 PM
To: Maverick Hamline <yomomluvsme@theeservice.com>;
<rebelluvshismom@electronicstorks.com>
Subject: RE: RE: My FRIGGIN Dad!

i swear, bruh. do you not understand sarcasm? i'm like a dad. not a dad. geez!

From: Maverick Hamline
Sent: Thursday, March 26, 2020 3:46 PM
To: Wiley Rougy <yafavboi@onlinedelivery.com>;
<rebelluvshismom@electronicstorks.com>
Subject: RE: RE: RE: My FRIGGIN Dad!

i mean wit u and tammy u never know, dude. how r you like a dad?

From: Wiley Rougy
Sent: Thursday, March 26, 2020 3:47 PM
To: Maverick Hamline <yomomluvsme@theeservice.com>;
<rebelluvshismom@electronicstorks.com>
Subject: RE: RE: RE: RE: My FRIGGIN Dad!

dads email. that's basically all they do. but i guess u wouldn't know. boom, sucka. and don't worry about me and tammy.

From: Maverick Hamline
Sent: Thursday, March 26, 2020 3:48 PM
To: Wiley Rougy <yafavboi@onlinedelivery.com>;
<rebelluvshismom@electronicstorks.com>
Subject: RE: RE: RE: RE: RE: My FRIGGIN Dad!

watever. sorry that my dad died. thanks dude. u should just b glad im so bored i was willin to read ur pervy lookin message. real talk tho. ur dad is nuts. wat did u do this time? not recycle ur soda can?

From: Maverick Hamline
Sent: Thursday, March 26, 2020 3:48 PM
To: Wiley Rougy <yafavboi@onlinedelivery.com>;
<rebelluvshismom@electronicstorks.com>
Subject: RE: RE: RE: RE: RE: RE: My FRIGGIN Dad!

or howl at some helmet wearin kid riding his bike down the sidewalk?

From: Maverick Hamline
Sent: Thursday, March 26, 2020 3:48 PM
To: Wiley Rougy <yafavboi@onlinedelivery.com>;
<rebelluvshismom@electronicstorks.com>
Subject: RE: RE: RE: RE: RE: RE: RE: My FRIGGIN Dad!

or snap at ur bug-eyed cat again?

From: Wiley Rougy
Sent: Thursday, March 26, 2020 3:53 PM
To: Maverick Hamline <yomomluvsme@theeservice.com>;
<rebelluvshismom@electronicstorks.com>
Subject: RE: RE: RE: RE: RE: RE: RE: RE: My FRIGGIN Dad!

bruh, chillax. that cat got "hit by a car" like 3 weeks ago. and i didn't
do anything. that's why i'm sooo pissed! i HATE having to spend
spring break here.

From: Maverick Hamline
Sent: Thursday, March 26, 2020 4:00 PM
To: Wiley Rougy <yafavboi@onlinedelivery.com>;
<rebelluvshismom@electronicstorks.com>
Subject: RE: RE: RE: RE: RE: RE: RE: RE: RE: My FRIGGIN Dad!

but wat happened tho?

From: Wiley Rougy
Sent: Thursday, March 26, 2020 4:10 PM
To: Maverick Hamline <yomomluvsme@theeservice.com>;
<rebelluvshismom@electronicstorks.com>
Subject: RE: RE: RE: RE: RE: RE: RE: RE: RE: My FRIGGIN Dad!

he basically went on sum straight-up psycho rant about how my
phone is "polluting" my mind. like okay, bruh? chill. but he was just
getting started. his next breath, he was on that werewolf motto
crap about "the family that kills together stays together," telling me
that he's tired. tired of stalking deer by himself. tired of pulling stray
pups by himself. tired of sneaking chickens from old man frank's
farm by himself. just rambling over and over. when it sounded like
he was about to finally shut up, he started back in about frank. like
who cares about friggin old frank? dude is like 150 and can barely
walk. anyways, dad started listing crap again. how old frank is such
a good dude. how he hates taking from him all the time. how he is
afraid he'll get caught and... blah blah blah. i told him to go take a
nap if he's tired. i mean, isn't that what he should do? if he doesn't
want to hunt so much, he should have thought about that before he
decided to have cubids. or better yet, he should just let me and faye
stay with mom all the time. mom has so much friggin money that
she can buy us food from wherever it is she buys it from. what really
set him off is when i told him to just go eat faye if he's so hungry. he
yanked MY phone out of my hands and threw it down on the friggin

floor. the whole thing shattered everywhere. like, bruh, it's deader than my grandma, and she's been dead since i was 3. like wtf? and then he ran out the friggin door.

From: Maverick Hamline
Sent: Thursday, March 26, 2020 4:16 PM
To: Wiley Rougy <yafavboi@onlinedelivery.com>;
<rebelluvshismom@electronicstorks.com>
Subject: RE: RE: RE: RE: RE: RE: RE: RE: RE: RE:... My FRIGGIN Dad!

dang son. billy joe don't play. faye is cool. whyd u throw her under the bus like that?

From: Wiley Rougy
Sent: Thursday, March 26, 2020 4:17 PM
To: Maverick Hamline <yomomluvsme@theeservice.com>;
<rebelluvshismom@electronicstorks.com>
Subject: RE: RE: RE: RE: RE: RE: RE: RE: RE: RE:... My FRIGGIN Dad!

i wasn't seriously telling him to go eat my sister!

From: Maverick Hamline
Sent: Thursday, March 26, 2020 4:18 PM
To: Wiley Rougy <yafavboi@onlinedelivery.com>;
<rebelluvshismom@electronicstorks.com>
Subject: RE: RE: RE: RE: RE: RE: RE: RE: RE: RE:... My FRIGGIN Dad!

that blows about ur grandma. btw wat is a cubid?

From: Wiley Rougy
Sent: Thursday, March 26, 2020 4:19 PM
To: Maverick Hamline <yomomluvsme@theeservice.com>;
<rebelluvshismom@electronicstorks.com>
Subject: RE: RE: RE: RE: RE: RE: RE: RE: RE: RE:... My FRIGGIN Dad!

bruh, a cub/kid. wtf! how do u not know that? and who cares about my friggin grandma? it's not like i even remember her.

From: Maverick Hamline
Sent: Thursday, March 26, 2020 4:21 PM
To: Wiley Rougy <yafavboi@onlinedelivery.com>;
<rebelluvshismom@electronicstorks.com>
Subject: RE: RE: RE: RE: RE: RE: RE: RE: RE: RE:... My FRIGGIN Dad!

oh. ok. well me mom and becca hunt together. its kinda fun. we usually can get a pigeon or 2 for dinner. but we cant really get any big animals.

From: Wiley Rougy
Sent: Thursday, March 26, 2020 4:22 PM
To: Maverick Hamline <yomomluvsme@theeservice.com>; <rebelluvshismom@electronicstorks.com>
Subject: RE: RE: RE: RE: RE: RE: RE: RE: RE: RE:... My FRIGGIN Dad!

of course u think it's fun. U R SUCH A LOSER! and the reason u only get a pigeon is cuz u all r 2 loud. real talk tho. don't none of u look 2 hungry 2 me. must be some fat pigeons.

From: Maverick Hamline
Sent: Thursday, March 26, 2020 4:25 PM
To: Wiley Rougy <yafavboi@onlinedelivery.com>; <rebelluvshismom@electronicstorks.com>
Subject: RE: RE: RE: RE: RE: RE: RE: RE: RE: RE:... My FRIGGIN Dad!

we just got good jeans.

From: Wiley Rougy
Sent: Thursday, March 26, 2020 4:25 PM
To: Maverick Hamline <yomomluvsme@theeservice.com>; <rebelluvshismom@electronicstorks.com>
Subject: RE: RE: RE: RE: RE: RE: RE: RE: RE: RE:... My FRIGGIN Dad!

haha. u idiot. u mean genes.

From: Maverick Hamline
Sent: Thursday, March 26, 2020 4:30 PM
To: Wiley Rougy <yafavboi@onlinedelivery.com>; <rebelluvshismom@electronicstorks.com>
Subject: RE: RE: RE: RE: RE: RE: RE: RE: RE: RE:... My FRIGGIN Dad!

forgot i am talking to a genius.

From: Wiley Rougy
Sent: Thursday, March 26, 2020 4:31 PM
To: Maverick Hamline <yomomluvsme@theeservice.com>; <rebelluvshismom@electronicstorks.com>
Subject: RE: RE: RE: RE: RE: RE: RE: RE: RE: RE:... My FRIGGIN Dad!

u know it.

From: Wiley Rougy
Sent: Thursday, March 26, 2020 5:00 PM
To: Maverick Hamline <yomomluvsme@theeservice.com>;
<rebelluvshismom@electronicstorks.com>
Subject: RE: RE: RE: RE: RE: RE: RE: RE: RE: RE:... My FRIGGIN Dad!

how r u going to play me like that? u just going to stop in the
middle of our convo?

From: Wiley Rougy
Sent: Thursday, March 26, 2020 5:25 PM
To: Maverick Hamline <yomomluvsme@theeservice.com>;
<rebelluvshismom@electronicstorks.com>
Subject: RE: RE: RE: RE: RE: RE: RE: RE: RE: RE:... My FRIGGIN Dad!

seriously? r u mad?

From: Maverick Hamline
Sent: Thursday, March 26, 2020 5:26 PM
To: Wiley Rougy <yafavboi@onlinedelivery.com>;
<rebelluvshismom@electronicstorks.com>
Subject: RE: RE: RE: RE: RE: RE: RE: RE: RE: RE:... My FRIGGIN Dad!

sorry dude. reb wouldnt stop textin til i answered him.

From: Wiley Rougy
Sent: Thursday, March 26, 2020 5:28 PM
To: Maverick Hamline <yomomluvsme@theeservice.com>;
<rebelluvshismom@electronicstorks.com>
Subject: RE: RE: RE: RE: RE: RE: RE: RE: RE: RE:... My FRIGGIN Dad!

wth is rebel anyway? does he not know how to read his email? like
seriously?

From: Maverick Hamline
Sent: Thursday, March 26, 2020 5:34 PM
To: Wiley Rougy <yafavboi@onlinedelivery.com>;
<rebelluvshismom@electronicstorks.com>
Subject: RE: RE: RE: RE: RE: RE: RE: RE: RE: RE:... My FRIGGIN Dad!

dude he doesnt even have an email account.

From: Wiley Rougy
Sent: Thursday, March 26, 2020 5:46 PM

To: Maverick Hamline <yomomluvsme@theeservice.com>;
<rebelluvshismom@electronicstorks.com>
Subject: RE: RE: RE: RE: RE: RE: RE: RE: RE: RE:... My FRIGGIN Dad!

what do u mean? who else have i been emailing then?

From: Maverick Hamline
Sent: Thursday, March 26, 2020 6:06 PM
To: Wiley Rougy <yafavboi@onlinedelivery.com>;
<rebelluvshismom@electronicstorks.com>
Subject: RE: RE: RE: RE: RE: RE: RE: RE: RE: RE:... My FRIGGIN Dad!

???

From: Wiley Rougy
Sent: Thursday, March 26, 2020 6:07 PM
To: Maverick Hamline <yomomluvsme@theeservice.com>;
<rebelluvshismom@electronicstorks.com>
Subject: RE: RE: RE: RE: RE: RE: RE: RE: RE: RE:... My FRIGGIN Dad!

well u would think the lame-o i've been emailing about MY personal
life would say something. like who does that?

From: Maverick Hamline
Sent: Thursday, March 26, 2020 6:07 PM
To: Wiley Rougy <yafavboi@onlinedelivery.com>;
<rebelluvshismom@electronicstorks.com>
Subject: RE: RE: RE: RE: RE: RE: RE: RE: RE: RE:... My FRIGGIN Dad!

i dunno dude.

From: Wiley Rougy
Sent: Thursday, March 26, 2020 6:08 PM
To: Maverick Hamline <yomomluvsme@theeservice.com>
Subject: RE: RE: RE: RE: RE: RE: RE: RE: RE: RE:... My FRIGGIN Dad!

what did reb say?

From: Maverick Hamline
Sent: Thursday, March 26, 2020 6:11 PM
To: Wiley Rougy <yafavboi@onlinedelivery.com>;
Subject: RE: RE: RE: RE: RE: RE: RE: RE: RE: RE:... My FRIGGIN Dad!

somethin about some video his mom took at the chicken barn. he
just sent it 2 me. musta finally got on some wi-fi. hang on...

From: Wiley Rougy
Sent: Thursday, March 26, 2020 6:12 PM
To: Maverick Hamline <yomomluvsme@theeservice.com>
Subject: RE: RE: RE: RE: RE: RE: RE: RE: RE: RE:... My FRIGGIN Dad!

probably something stupid. he is 2 close 2 his mom. weird.

From: Wiley Rougy
Sent: Thursday, March 26, 2020 6:20 PM
To: Maverick Hamline <yomomluvsme@theeservice.com>
Subject: RE: RE: RE: RE: RE: RE: RE: RE: RE: RE:... My FRIGGIN Dad!

hello? am i bein ignored again?

From: Wiley Rougy
Sent: Thursday, March 26, 2020 6:45 PM
To: Maverick Hamline <yomomluvsme@theeservice.com>
Subject: RE: RE: RE: RE: RE: RE: RE: RE: RE: RE:... My FRIGGIN Dad!

did ur mom go all billy joe and take ur phone?

From: Wiley Rougy
Sent: Thursday, March 26, 2020 7:15 PM
To: Maverick Hamline <yomomluvsme@theeservice.com>
Subject: RE: RE: RE: RE: RE: RE: RE: RE: RE: RE:... My FRIGGIN Dad!

mav, where u at, bruh?

From: Wiley Rougy
Sent: Thursday, March 26, 2020 7:55 PM
To: Maverick Hamline <yomomluvsme@theeservice.com>
Subject: RE: RE: RE: RE: RE: RE: RE: RE: RE: RE:... My FRIGGIN Dad!

helllllooooooooooooooooooooooooooo?

From: Maverick Hamline
Sent: Thursday, March 26, 2020 10:52 PM
To: Wiley Rougy <yafavboi@onlinedelivery.com>;
Subject: RE: RE: RE: RE: RE: RE: RE: RE: RE: RE:... My FRIGGIN Dad!

sorry. was watchin the video.

From: Wiley Rougy
Sent: Thursday, March 26, 2020 10:54 PM
To: Maverick Hamline <yomomluvsme@theeservice.com>

Subject: RE: RE: RE: RE: RE: RE: RE: RE: RE: RE:... My FRIGGIN Dad!

is it 4 hours long? gah.

From: Maverick Hamline
Sent: Thursday, March 26, 2020 10:55 PM
To: Wiley Rougy <yafavboi@onlinedelivery.com>;
Subject: RE: RE: RE: RE: RE: RE: RE: RE: RE: RE:... My FRIGGIN Dad!

i had to make sure i was seein right. promise u wont freak out but i need to tell u sumthin dude.

From: Wiley Rougy
Sent: Thursday, March 26, 2020 10:56 PM
To: Maverick Hamline <yomomluvsme@theeservice.com>
Subject: RE: RE: RE: RE: RE: RE: RE: RE: RE: RE:... My FRIGGIN Dad!

ok. fine.

From: Maverick Hamline
Sent: Thursday, March 26, 2020 10:56 PM
To: Wiley Rougy <yafavboi@onlinedelivery.com>;
Subject: RE: RE: RE: RE: RE: RE: RE: RE: RE: RE:... My FRIGGIN Dad!

im serious.

From: Wiley Rougy
Sent: Thursday, March 26, 2020 10:57 PM
To: Maverick Hamline <yomomluvsme@theeservice.com>
Subject: RE: RE: RE: RE: RE: RE: RE: RE: RE: RE:... My FRIGGIN Dad!

i said fine.

From: Maverick Hamline
Sent: Thursday, March 26, 2020 10:58 PM
To: Wiley Rougy <yafavboi@onlinedelivery.com>;
Subject: RE: RE: RE: RE: RE: RE: RE: RE: RE: RE:... My FRIGGIN Dad!

alright. but it involves u.

From: Wiley Rougy
Sent: Thursday, March 26, 2020 10:58 PM
To: Maverick Hamline <yomomluvsme@theeservice.com>
Subject: RE: RE: RE: RE: RE: RE: RE: RE: RE: RE:... My FRIGGIN Dad!

me? STOP BEING SHADY, bruh. tell me what u r seein.

From: Maverick Hamline
Sent: Thursday, March 26, 2020 11:01 PM
To: Wiley Rougy <yafavboi@onlinedelivery.com>;
Subject: RE: RE: RE: RE: RE: RE: RE: RE: RE: RE:... My FRIGGIN Dad!

ok. its all in the vid. im goin 2 email u a link 2 it. www.
vidcapsonmobile.com/vids/168997146777

From: Maverick Hamline
Sent: Thursday, March 26, 2020 11:08 PM
To: Wiley Rougy <yafavboi@onlinedelivery.com>;
Subject: RE: RE: RE: RE: RE: RE: RE: RE: RE: RE:... My FRIGGIN Dad!

did u watch it yet?

From: Maverick Hamline
Sent: Thursday, March 26, 2020 11:15 PM
To: Wiley Rougy <yafavboi@onlinedelivery.com>;
Subject: RE: RE: RE: RE: RE: RE: RE: RE: RE: RE:... My FRIGGIN Dad!

dude i cant show u sumthin like that and then u go all radio silent
on me. did u watch it yet?

From: Wiley Rougy
Sent: Thursday, March 26, 2020 11:23 PM
To: Maverick Hamline <yomomluvsme@theeservice.com>
Subject: RE: RE: RE: RE: RE: RE: RE: RE: RE: RE:... My FRIGGIN Dad!

give me a FRIGGIN minute! r u sure it's 4 real?

From: Maverick Hamline
Sent: Thursday, March 26, 2020 11:26 PM
To: Wiley Rougy <yafavboi@onlinedelivery.com>;
Subject: RE: RE: RE: RE: RE: RE: RE: RE: RE: RE:... My FRIGGIN Dad!

its from rebels mom. we both know she didnt fake it. she can barely
text much less create some kind of blood spurtin visual effects
hollywood level murder scene.

From: Wiley Rougy
Sent: Thursday, March 26, 2020 11:27 PM
To: Maverick Hamline <yomomluvsme@theeservice.com>
Subject: RE: RE: RE: RE: RE: RE: RE: RE: RE: RE:... My FRIGGIN Dad!

when?

From: Maverick Hamline
Sent: Thursday, March 26, 2020 11:28 PM
To: Wiley Rougy <yafavboi@onlinedelivery.com>;
Subject: RE: RE: RE: RE: RE: RE: RE: RE: RE: RE:... My FRIGGIN Dad!

when wat? dude wat r u even talkin about?

From: Wiley Rougy
Sent: Thursday, March 26, 2020 11:28 PM
To: Maverick Hamline <yomomluvsme@theeservice.com>
Subject: RE: RE: RE: RE: RE: RE: RE: RE: RE:... My FRIGGIN Dad!

WHEN DID SHE TAKE THE VID?!? come on, bruh. use ur brain.

From: Maverick Hamline
Sent: Thursday, March 26, 2020 11:30 PM
To: Wiley Rougy <yafavboi@onlinedelivery.com>;
Subject: RE: RE: RE: RE: RE: RE: RE: RE: RE: RE:... My FRIGGIN Dad!

look I know u r upset but im tryin to help u.

From: Wiley Rougy
Sent: Thursday, March 26, 2020 11:32 PM
To: Maverick Hamline <yomomluvsme@theeservice.com>
Subject: RE: RE: RE: RE: RE: RE: RE: RE: RE:... My FRIGGIN Dad!

it would help me if i knew when she took the video.

From: Maverick Hamline
Sent: Thursday, March 26, 2020 11:33 PM
To: Wiley Rougy <yafavboi@onlinedelivery.com>;
Subject: RE: RE: RE: RE: RE: RE: RE: RE: RE: RE:... My FRIGGIN Dad!

let me text reb. brb.

From: Maverick Hamline
Sent: Thursday, March 26, 2020 11:41 PM
To: Wiley Rougy <yafavboi@onlinedelivery.com>;
Subject: RE: RE: RE: RE: RE: RE: RE: RE: RE: RE:... My FRIGGIN Dad!

from him... IDK exactly, but it was probably 30 minutes ago. Mom
said she was in the back of the chicken barn and saw Wiley's dad
rip Mr. Frank's arm off his friggin body. Mom is an OG, so she pulled
her phone out and started taping it so she'd have proof. Then, when
she had enough footage, she flew out that coop and left the door

up for those chickens. She had to give them birds a chance to save themselves. She loves them. -Rebel

From: Wiley Rougy
Sent: Thursday, March 26, 2020 11:42 PM
To: Maverick Hamline <yomomluvsme@theeservice.com>
Subject: RE: RE: RE: RE: RE: RE: RE: RE: RE: RE:... My FRIGGIN Dad!

what does he mean so she'd have proof?

From: Maverick Hamline
Sent: Thursday, March 26, 2020 11:43 PM
To: Wiley Rougy <yafavboi@onlinedelivery.com>;
Subject: RE: RE: RE: RE: RE: RE: RE: RE: RE: RE:... My FRIGGIN Dad!

of ur dad murderin old man frank, i guess??? i dunno dude!

From: Maverick Hamline
Sent: Thursday, March 26, 2020 11:44 PM
To: Wiley Rougy <yafavboi@onlinedelivery.com>;
Subject: RE: RE: RE: RE: RE: RE: RE: RE: RE: RE:... My FRIGGIN Dad!

im sure she is on the schedule or watever 2 b at work. shed obviously b the 1st suspect.

From: Wiley Rougy
Sent: Thursday, March 26, 2020 11:45 PM
To: Maverick Hamline <yomomluvsme@theeservice.com>
Subject: RE: RE: RE: RE: RE: RE: RE: RE: RE: RE:... My FRIGGIN Dad!

like anybody would suspect her of killing anybody. please. only by boring somebody to death. what do we do?

From: Maverick Hamline
Sent: Thursday, March 26, 2020 11:45 PM
To: Wiley Rougy <yafavboi@onlinedelivery.com>;
Subject: RE: RE: RE: RE: RE: RE: RE: RE: RE: RE:... My FRIGGIN Dad!

nothin.

From: Wiley Rougy
Sent: Thursday, March 26, 2020 11:45 PM
To: Maverick Hamline <yomomluvsme@theeservice.com>
Subject: RE: RE: RE: RE: RE: RE: RE: RE: RE: RE:... My FRIGGIN Dad!

come again?

From: Wiley Rougy
Sent: Thursday, March 26, 2020 11:48 PM
To: Maverick Hamline <yomomluvsme@theeservice.com>
Subject: RE: RE: RE: RE: RE: RE: RE: RE: RE: RE:... My FRIGGIN Dad!

HELLLOOOOOOOOOOOOOOOOOOO?!?

From: Maverick Hamline
Sent: Thursday, March 26, 2020 11:51 PM
To: Wiley Rougy <yafavboi@onlinedelivery.com>;
Subject: RE: RE: RE: RE: RE: RE: RE: RE: RE: RE:... My FRIGGIN Dad!

wat i just said. u can read. WE arent doin NOTHIN.

From: Wiley Rougy
Sent: Thursday, March 26, 2020 11:52 PM
To: Maverick Hamline <yomomluvsme@theeservice.com>
Subject: RE: RE: RE: RE: RE: RE: RE: RE: RE: RE:... My FRIGGIN Dad!

bruh, u r 4 REAL trying my patience. u need 2 pay more attention
in school. if "WE arent doin NOTHIN," that means we r doing
something. so what r we doing?

From: Wilcy Rougy
Sent: Thursday, March 26, 2020 11:52 PM
To: Maverick Hamline <yomomluvsme@theeservice.com>
Subject: RE: RE: RE: RE: RE: RE: RE: RE: RE: RE:... My FRIGGIN Dad!

my dad could go to jail or worse!!!

From: Maverick Hamline
Sent: Thursday, March 26, 2020 11:55 PM
To: Wiley Rougy <yafavboi@onlinedelivery.com>;
Subject: RE: RE: RE: RE: RE: RE: RE: RE: RE: RE:... My FRIGGIN Dad!

DUDE!!!! UR FRIGGIN DAD just murdered an old man who was
inside his OWN chicken barn. wolves dont murder humans. all
werewolves know that. even the dumb ones. even the reallllllllll
dumb ones. we ALL know that from birth.

From: Maverick Hamline
Sent: Thursday, March 26, 2020 11:55 PM

To: Wiley Rougy <yafavboi@onlinedelivery.com>;
Subject: RE: RE: RE: RE: RE: RE: RE: RE: RE: RE:... My FRIGGIN Dad!

and dude. ur dads not dumb.

From: Maverick Hamline
Sent: Thursday, March 26, 2020 11:56 PM
To: Wiley Rougy <yafavboi@onlinedelivery.com>;
Subject: RE: RE: RE: RE: RE: RE: RE: RE: RE: RE:... My FRIGGIN Dad!

Just to be extra clear, WE are not doing anything. (I hope my proper
language is a little easier for someone as smart as you to reed.)

From: Wiley Rougy
Sent: Thursday, March 26, 2020 11:57 PM
To: Maverick Hamline <yomomluvsme@theeservice.com>
Subject: RE: RE: RE: RE: RE: RE: RE: RE: RE: RE:... My FRIGGIN Dad!

u r so friggin dramatic. btw, you misspelled read. im sure there has 2
b a reason he killed him. maybe frank tried 2 murder him first?

From: Maverick Hamline
Sent: Thursday, March 26, 2020 11:58 PM
To: Wiley Rougy <yafavboi@onlinedelivery.com>;
Subject: RE: RE: RE: RE: RE: RE: RE: RE: RE: RE:... My FRIGGIN Dad!

omg!!!! who cares about spellin?!!!!!

From: Maverick Hamline
Sent: Thursday, March 26, 2020 11:58 PM
To: Wiley Rougy <yafavboi@onlinedelivery.com>;
Subject: RE: RE: RE: RE: RE: RE: RE: RE: RE: RE:... My FRIGGIN Dad!

dude, u said urself that ur dad is a psycho. did u not watch the
friggin video?

From: Wiley Rougy
Sent: Friday, March 27, 2020 12:00 AM
To: Maverick Hamline <yomomluvsme@theeservice.com>
Subject: RE: RE: RE: RE: RE: RE: RE: RE: RE: RE:... My FRIGGIN Dad!

YES, BRUH. I WATCHED THE FRIGGIN VIDEO!

From: Maverick Hamline
Sent: Friday, March 27, 2020 12:01AM

To: Wiley Rougy <yafavboi@onlinedelivery.com>;
Subject: RE: RE: RE: RE: RE: RE: RE: RE: RE: RE:... My FRIGGIN Dad!

did u listen 2 it 2?

From: Wiley Rougy
Sent: Friday, March 27, 2020 12:01 AM
To: Maverick Hamline <yomomluvsme@theeservice.com>
Subject: RE: RE: RE: RE: RE: RE: RE: RE: RE: RE:... My FRIGGIN Dad!

no. faye is sleeping. it is midnight u know.

From: Maverick Hamline
Sent: Friday, March 27, 2020 12:05 AM
To: Wiley Rougy <yafavboi@onlinedelivery.com>;
Subject: RE: RE: RE: RE: RE: RE: RE: RE: RE: RE:... My FRIGGIN Dad!

well mr genius ur dad admitted ON THE FRIGGIN VIDEO that he
was at the barn 2 take a bunch of franks chickens cuz he was tired
of always havin 2 hunt. said he couldnt do it anymore. frank said he
was callin the police. ur dad yanked his phone and chunked it on
the ground. i guess thats like his thing or watever. and he ripped
franks friggin arm off and killed him.

From: Wiley Rougy
Sent: Friday, March 27, 2020 12:07 AM
To: Maverick Hamline <yomomluvsme@theeservice.com>
Subject: RE: RE: RE: RE: RE: RE: RE: RE: RE: RE:... My FRIGGIN Dad!

r u sure? is all that 4 real said on the video?

From: Maverick Hamline
Sent: Friday, March 27, 2020 12:08 AM
To: Wiley Rougy <yafavboi@onlinedelivery.com>;
Subject: RE: RE: RE: RE: RE: RE: RE: RE: RE: RE:... My FRIGGIN Dad!

yes dude along with a bunch of other freaky stuff. like imma lie
about that.

From: Wiley Rougy
Sent: Friday, March 27, 2020 12:08 AM
To: Maverick Hamline <yomomluvsme@theeservice.com>
Subject: RE: RE: RE: RE: RE: RE: RE: RE: RE: RE:... My FRIGGIN Dad!

what do we do?

From: Maverick Hamline
Sent: Friday, March 27, 2020 12:09 AM
To: Wiley Rougy <yafavboi@onlinedelivery.com>;
Subject: RE: RE: RE: RE: RE: RE: RE: RE: RE: RE:... My FRIGGIN Dad!

hang on a sec. reb is textin me again.

From: Wiley Rougy
Sent: Friday, March 27, 2020 12:09 AM
To: Maverick Hamline <yomomluvsme@theeservice.com>
Subject: RE: RE: RE: RE: RE: RE: RE: RE: RE: RE:... My FRIGGIN Dad!

what is he saying?

From: Wiley Rougy
Sent: Friday, March 27, 2020 12:10 AM
To: Maverick Hamline <yomomluvsme@theeservice.com>
Subject: RE: RE: RE: RE: RE: RE: RE: RE: RE: RE:... My FRIGGIN Dad!

come on, bruh. don't leave me hanging?

From: Wiley Rougy
Sent: Friday, March 27, 2020 12:10 AM
To: Maverick Hamline <yomomluvsme@theeservice.com>
Subject: RE: RE: RE: RE: RE: RE: RE: RE: RE: RE:... My FRIGGIN Dad!

maverick, what's he saying?

From: Maverick Hamline
Sent: Friday, March 27, 2020 12:12 AM
To: Wiley Rougy <yafavboi@onlinedelivery.com>;
Subject: RE: RE: RE: RE: RE: RE: RE: RE: RE: RE:... My FRIGGIN Dad!

im sorry dude but the police have ur dad. rebs mom is talking 2 them now.

From: Wiley Rougy
Sent: Friday, March 27, 2020 12:14 AM
To: Maverick Hamline <yomomluvsme@theeservice.com>
Subject: RE: RE: RE: RE: RE: RE: RE: RE: RE: RE:... My FRIGGIN Dad!

but we have 2 do something. u know what the punishment is for a werewolf killing a human.

From: Maverick Hamline

Sent: Friday, March 27, 2020 12:14 AM
To: Wiley Rougy <yafavboi@onlinedelivery.com>;
Subject: RE: RE: RE: RE: RE: RE: RE: RE: RE: RE:... My FRIGGIN Dad!

im sorry dude. i really am.

From: Wiley Rougy
Sent: Friday, March 27, 2020 12:15 AM
To: Maverick Hamline <yomomluvsme@theeservice.com>
Subject: RE: RE: RE: RE: RE: RE: RE: RE: RE: RE:... My FRIGGIN Dad!

there has 2 be something we can do.

From: Maverick Hamline
Sent: Friday, March 27, 2020 12:16 AM
To: Wiley Rougy <yafavboi@onlinedelivery.com>;
Subject: RE: RE: RE: RE: RE: RE: RE: RE: RE: RE:... My FRIGGIN Dad!

theres nothin 2 be done. gotta go tho. my mom is callin 4 me and
becca. gotta hunt if we want 2 eat.

From: Wiley Rougy
Sent: Friday, March 27, 2020 12:17 AM
To: Maverick Hamline <yomomluvsme@theeservice.com>
Subject: RE: RE: RE: RE: RE: RE: RE: RE: RE: RE:... My FRIGGIN Dad!

u can't be serious. my dad is in all kinds of trouble and u are worried
about urself. typical.

From: Maverick Hamline
Sent: Friday, March 27, 2020 12:18 AM
To: Wiley Rougy <yafavboi@onlinedelivery.com>;
Subject: RE: RE: RE: RE: RE: RE: RE: RE: RE: RE:... My FRIGGIN Dad!

sorry dude. but we live by the motto. the family that kills together
stays together. mom is serious about it.

From: Wiley Rougy
Sent: Friday, March 27, 2020 12:19 AM
To: Maverick Hamline <yomomluvsme@theeservice.com>
Subject: RE: RE: RE: RE: RE: RE: RE: RE: RE: RE:... My FRIGGIN Dad!

oh i see how it is. whatever. just go do u, bruh. don't worry about me.
or about faye. or about my dad. or about anybody but urself and ur
weirdo family. enjoy ur friggin pigeon.

From: Maverick Hamline
Sent: Friday, March 27, 2020 12:20 AM
To: Wiley Rougy <yafavboi@onlinedelivery.com>;
Subject: RE: RE: RE: RE: RE: RE: RE: RE: RE: RE:... My FRIGGIN Dad!

my weirdo family? watever. dude all u do is talk crap about everybody but urself and im tired of it.

From: Maverick Hamline
Sent: Friday, March 27, 2020 12:20 AM
To: Wiley Rougy <yafavboi@onlinedelivery.com>;
Subject: RE: RE: RE: RE: RE: RE: RE: RE: RE: RE:... My FRIGGIN Dad!

oh and just for the record i FRIGGIN luv pigeons!

From: Wiley Rougy
Sent: Friday, March 27, 2020 12:21 AM
To: Maverick Hamline <yomomluvsme@theeservice.com>
Subject: RE: RE: RE: RE: RE: RE: RE: RE: RE: RE:... My FRIGGIN Dad!

whatever.

From: Wiley Rougy
Sent: Friday, March 27, 2020 2:30 PM
To: Maverick Hamline <yomomluvsme@theeservice.com>
Subject: RE: RE: RE: RE: RE: RE: RE: RE: RE: RE:... My FRIGGIN Dad!

i'm still waiting 2 hear from dad. u get some fat pigeons last night, bruh?

From: Wiley Rougy
Sent: Friday, March 27, 2020 6:43 PM
To: Maverick Hamline <yomomluvsme@theeservice.com>
Subject: RE: RE: RE: RE: RE: RE: RE: RE: RE: RE:... My FRIGGIN Dad!

mav? u don't think it's my fault, do u?

From: Wiley Rougy
Sent: Friday, March 27, 2020 8:30 PM
To: Maverick Hamline <yomomluvsme@theeservice.com>
Subject: RE: RE: RE: RE: RE: RE: RE: RE: RE: RE:... My FRIGGIN Dad!

mav? u there? i don't know what to do. faye's hungry. me 2 actually. i don't know how 2 hunt.

From: Wiley Rougy
Sent: Saturday, March 28, 2020 10:33 am
To: Maverick Hamline <yomomluvsme@theeservice.com>
Subject: RE: RE: RE: RE: RE: RE: RE: RE: RE: RE:... My FRIGGIN Dad!

mav? come on. where u at? i need you, bruh.

From: Wiley Rougy
Sent: Saturday, March 28, 2020 11:49 am
To: Maverick Hamline <yomomluvsme@theeservice.com>
Subject: RE: RE: RE: RE: RE: RE: RE: RE: RE: RE:... My FRIGGIN Dad!

do u know my mom's number? i don't know how to get in touch
with her. she doesn't email.

From: Wiley Rougy
Sent: Saturday, March 28, 2020 7:16 PM
To: Maverick Hamline <yomomluvsme@theeservice.com>
Subject: RE: RE: RE: RE: RE: RE: RE: RE: RE: RE:... My FRIGGIN Dad!

4 real, mav? u ignoring me?

From: Mail Failure Systems
Sent: Saturday, March 28, 2020 7:21 PM
To: Wiley Rougy <yafavboi@onlinedelivery.com>
Subject: Delivery of Failed Mail Notification

Your message to yomomluvsme@theeservice.com failed because
the addressee no longer wishes to receive messages from
yafavboi@onlinedelivery.com.

To learn more, click here.

# FROM HIEMSLANDIA

**M**IKI WAS TWIRLING ATOP AN ice cube when Vida first saw him. Each time he leapt off the edge with his fist in the air, her heart followed. Perhaps it was too soon, but she couldn't help it. She'd heard the stories about the children from Hiemslandia. The ice thieves. The giants. And the rescue—of course the rescue. Even with the condensation droplets in the way, Vida could see Miki's wounded eyes shining through the chilled glass.

Vida sat down at his empty table and smiled. And Miki sat down on the ice and looked back at her. He extended his arm to the foggy covering and polished it with his sleeve. His action was nothing. But Vida, seeing his openness toward her, giggled and loosened her shoulders.

"How are you?" she asked.

"A little warm, and I'm thinking about the giants. But I'm okay. I guess," he replied through a tiny blue straw, with his voice barely that of a whisper.

Warm? She was wearing a sweater, a coat, and a scarf, and, still, her arm hairs tingled.

"I want to help you. Is that okay?"

Miki stood up and scratched at his chin. The ice cube rocked, but, instead of wobbling, his body swayed confidently with it.

He grabbed the straw again and spoke into it. "If you know how to."

She didn't hesitate when she slapped the buzzer on the corner of the table. "I'll take him!" she shouted. "I'll take him—Miki—now!"

The adoption mixer's hostess tottered to the table and pulled up a stool beside Vida.

"Are you sure?" she asked.

Vida looked over at the boy, who now was on his knees with his head turned down toward the ice, and her heart jumped again. "I think he's praying. I bet he's thanking God for me," she said to the hostess. Then, she took a deep breath and spoke softly. "I am sure," she said.

The hostess stared at Vida until Vida looked away.

"Very well," said the hostess. "I'll pack him securely for you, and I'll even toss in a couple of extra ice cubes from his home planet. He'll need to stay as cold as possible."

Vida watched as the hostess took Miki to the back. She hoped this would be the only time she would not be by her son's side.

"Good luck," the hostess said as Vida and the boy headed home. "I think you're going to need it."

And the door shut.

Vida shook her head. "What a strange woman," she whispered.

At home, Vida filled a glass pitcher with as many ice cubes as it would hold and poured a cup of water in it. Then, she grabbed Miki and placed him inside his new vessel.

"What do you think?" she asked, with her hands shaking against the glass.

His lips moved, but his voice wasn't strong enough to fill the empty room.

"Oops, sorry. I forgot something," she said, and she reached in her pocket to retrieve the same blue straw he'd had at the mixer.

"Let's try that again. What do you think?"

"It's spacious enough," he said. "May I have one of my cubes from home, though?"

"Of course, sweetie." She ran to the freezer to open the airtight package the hostess had given Vida as she was leaving.

She held the cube in her hand and lowered it to where her new son stood.

"Thank you," he said.

"You're welcome," she replied.

Vida smelled her hands. Hiemslandia. She closed her eyes and imagined her son's homeland. The azure ground. The water flowing under the ice. The horned beasts flying as if they were delicate birds. The miniscule people laughing and dancing. And then, as if she couldn't help herself, she saw the final days. Destruction. The giants who'd come. Their colossal feet breaking the ice—their homes. The bodies like naked splinters among the broken landscape. And worst of all: Miki's face before and after.

When she opened her eyes, it was dark.

"Let's talk more tomorrow," she said.

Vida took Miki and his container up the stairs and placed him on a towel on her nightstand. "I'll sleep here, so if you need anything, all you have to do is call me," she said. She added reassuringly, "I'm a light sleeper."

She sat on the edge of the bed and reached to turn off the lamp, and then it hit her. She'd forgotten something. She ran to the bathroom and returned with a pair of scissors. She picked up the pitcher from the nightstand and unfolded the towel. She cut off one of the corner's and folded it back perfectly. Vida's friends all talked about the joy of tucking their children in at night. She deserved this moment.

"Miki, sweetie, this blanket is for you. I know that you don't really get cold, but it might help you be more comfortable. If nothing else, you can rest your head on it," she said.

He grabbed the piece of cloth and nodded.

Vida crawled into her bed again, and this time she turned off the light.

Miki watched her sleep for the longest time. Then, he grabbed his blanket and folded it under his head. He was safe for now. He could sleep.

It was the light's rays that startled the boy. The giants. Were they back? Were they here to conquer all that remained of Hiemslandia? The heat scorched the back of his neck, and his delicate skin reddened, even under the protection of the pitcher's thick glass. He stood on the edge of his cube—the one from his home—and he glared into the light. He faced the heat. He ripped the blanket and wrapped it around his head. A bandana. A warrior. He would fight. He would stand his ground. The giants could kill him. They could crush his body. He'd seen it all before. But they couldn't defeat his spirit. They wouldn't. They couldn't.

The light's intensity increased by the second, but Miki didn't budge. His hands sat on his hip. The muscles in his face tightened, and his lips swelled.

And then, just as the light seemed to back down, the bedroom door squeaked. It was one of the giants.

He jumped from the pitcher and charged the enemy.

Miki's soaked, bare feet trekked across the nightstand and down the cracked drawers. Perched atop the last hurdle, he grabbed his straw and vaulted to the carpet. His feet smacked the surface, and his bones popped and throbbed. His tiny feet tackled the dirty fibers. He breathed deeper with each step. Dust flew up from beneath him, and stray fingernails knocked him over. Still, he rose and ran toward the giant.

The giant approached. Slowly and quietly, not knowing the battle had begun.

The toes of the giant towered Miki.

Closer and closer they came.

With each step, the heat from earth grew stronger and stronger. Sweat covered Miki's body so much that discerning between water and his own fluids was impossible.

Miki had one shot, so he took it.

With all his strength that remained, he dived into the giant's toes and ripped and roared.

The giant, in return, howled.

Miki collapsed. But as he lay sprawled on the bedroom carpet, he looked up and saw the giant retreating.

The boy had won. "For Hiemslandia," he whispered.

It didn't take long until he was with the ones from Hiemslandia again.

---

David had tried to be quiet when he entered the bedroom as the morning sun rose.

He knew about Miki, and he'd rushed to get back home. He—the new father—wanted to surprise his wife and his son, but he had stubbed his toe on something and had to go back to the switch to turn on the light.

Vida didn't seem alarmed when the lights came on. Instead, she looked at the pitcher.

"Good morning, sweetie," she said. "I want you to meet your dad."

Her eyes weren't playing tricks on her. He was gone.

"Miki! Miki!"

Vida and David got on their knees and crawled around the bedroom. It only took a few seconds to find him.

"Why would he get out of his pitcher?" she asked, cradling their son in her cupped palms. "Why would he leave his ice cubes? He knew better."

But then Vida noticed the boy's bandana.

# THE COMET SEEKERS

OLIVER WAS SCRUBBING CRUSTY GRAVY from his little brother's plate when he saw the comet shining through the scratched glass of the kitchen window, and he was gone before the plate sank to the bottom of the dirty dishwater.

He snatched the only two coats off the wooden hangers in the hallway closet and ran to his brother's bedroom, where he fumbled through a pile of clothes to find enough layers to keep the boy warm. A scarf and a thermal shirt. Gloves. He scooped them into his arms.

"Henry!" he shouted. "Henry!"

Socked feet raced from the dim-lit living room.

When Henry reached Oliver, Oliver grabbed the boy's shoulders and knelt before him. "Lift up your arms," he said, and the boy did so without any questions. Oliver shook as he covered the boy's body.

"He's back," Oliver finally said.

Henry clapped his hands and smiled. "He's back," he repeated as Oliver tightened the scarf around Henry's neck.

"We need to go see him," Oliver said, extending his hand. Henry took his brother's offering, and they ran into the forest.

———

"Pa!" Oliver cried. "Pa!" For a moment, he became the coyotes resting in the distance. Focused and broken, but mostly hungry. Henry was his echo—a learning pup. His voice soft—and then, even lighter until it was lost among the breeze.

The brothers ripped through the dying shrubbery. The branches crackled, and vines snapped. Oliver pulled Henry along. The young boy huffed loudly; his breaths became as thick as the fog nipping at his ankles.

Their feet stomped in the gathering snow. A new heaviness burdened each step.

"Pa!" Oliver called again. "Pa!" he couldn't stop calling. His voice was a song. It was a melody that he believed the stars and sky already knew.

The comet's glow pulsed in the sky. As the boys called it, it lived. It was a heart—both theirs and his. There was a time when they were the same.

Henry's tiny body plunged forward when he saw the comet's light. He arched his back, and his mouth opened. His arms moved like wings, flapping behind his body. "Pa!"

They reached the clearing and stopped. All that remained was a lonely, snow-covered oak tree.

———

Oliver watched Henry dart toward the tree. The boy howled as he ran; the sounds didn't stop as he jumped for the limbs—any, all, he would take whatever.

"Come back to us," he whispered.

Even a boy is old enough to understand defeat.

He sat on the snowy ground and began to cry.

———

Oliver looked on and waited—for anything.

When it didn't come, he listened to his brother's voice. "We're too far away, Oli," Henry said. "That's why he's not answering us."

Oliver gazed into the sky. When he turned back to Henry and spoke, his voice was different. "We have to get closer," he said.

Oliver ran at the tree and kicked it as soon as it was within reach. The bark didn't fall away when he pulled his boot back.

"Can you hold on to my back?" he asked.

Henry nodded furiously, wiping his eyes.

"You can't let go," Oliver said. "You can't, Henry. Do you understand?"

"I won't," he said. "I promise."

Oliver bent down for Henry to climb aboard his back, and Henry wrapped his arms around his brother's neck and moved his knees to his sides.

Oliver reached for the first limb and pulled. Then again. And again. Upward they went.

---

The brothers stood at the highest point in the snowy forest. So high that some of the birds looked at them enviously. "Pa!" Oliver called. "Pa, answer us!"

Henry watched his brother yell into the sky. The sounds were harsh and angry, but he didn't cover his ears. Instead, he slowly crawled off Oliver's back and joined him.

"Why won't he say anything?" Henry asked.

"I don't know," Oliver replied. "Maybe it's not him." He looked down at his baby brother.

Henry grabbed Oliver's hand and squeezed it. "It's him," he said. "But maybe we still aren't close enough." He pointed to the sky.

A tear rolled down Oliver's cheek. "Okay," he said to Henry. "But it has to be your decision. You have to decide."

"I've already decided," Henry said.

They grasped hands and leaped toward the stars.

---

When Oliver was seven, his pa took him stargazing on a hill. Oliver didn't care about the stars or the mysteries they contained, but he loved the man beside him.

"You don't know that one, do you?" his pa asked.

"Which one?"

The man sat up carefully and grabbed his son. He pulled the boy in closely and took his hand into his own. He squinted and pointed to the brightest star in the sky. "That one," he said.

Oliver leaned in and focused as hard as he could. "The shooting star?" he asked.

"That one, but it's not a shooting star."

Oliver was quiet.

"Shooting stars die. Comets—and that right there, son, is a comet—can last for hundreds and thousands of years."

"Thousands of years?" Oliver asked.

His pa nodded.

"Just because something can't be seen doesn't mean that it's gone. You see, comets come back," he said as his voice began to trail off into the damp air.

Oliver turned to face his pa, and when he did, the man he adored was crying. "There's something I have to tell you," he said. "I'm like that comet, Oli."

# THE MERPOD

**A**FTER INSISTING ON EXPANDING THE pod again, Herman brought Alice over on Saturday night to the abode that he shared with Olga and Elaine. Their home was rather plain—a jaggedly obtuse rock that jutted out of the foamy sea. It was coated in bird dung. Flies buzzed along the surface. There was barely enough room for the four of them. But the sea was roomy. There wasn't a mermaid or merman alive who could argue that. Plus, it was a warm rock and the perfect spot for dolphin watching.

Small talk circulated within the group. It was Herman who did most of the initial blabbing. Half of the things he said didn't make any sense. When Olga told him as much, he quieted down. "Sorry, old lady number one," he said, pinching her forearm. "Now, calm yourself." She rolled her eyes and scooted away.

With Herman quiet for a change, Alice took the floor. Nothing she added—not the talk about the family of vegetarian pelicans, the increased seashell theft, or the rumored live-action remake of *The Little Mermaid*—sparked much discussion until she brought up her interest in food. When she mentioned she was good at preparing meals, the merwives' tails nearly split their moonlit home into pebbles.

"You know food?!" Olga blurted.

"Oh, I haven't had a good breakfast in years," Elaine said. "Olga and I can barely clean seaweed."

"Yes," Olga spat. "That's true."

Herman rubbed his stomach. "I'm underfed," he said, chuckling. "Too skinny."

"If you'd raise a hand instead of relying on us to do all the work, you might have more to eat," Olga said.

The rock went quiet except for the sound from a stray, nearby splash. Only Elaine seemed to notice, but she didn't say anything.

Then Elaine, being Elaine, thought it best to end the night on a good note. She took the lead and insisted that she and Olga say goodnight. Elaine pecked Herman on the cheek. Olga waited and turned her attention to the curious lobster that inched toward Herman's tail.

After the two mermaids splashed into the warm, dingy water below, Elaine rose back above the surface and gave a thumbs-up to Herman.

Finally alone, Herman and Alice scooted closer together atop the rock. He inched his tail to hers, and the two finally touched. He was a little scaly, but, she figured, she could find a better time for a conversation about moisturizing techniques.

"Did you mean what you said earlier? About breakfast?" Herman asked.

"Of course," she said. "I love to make breakfast."

He didn't hesitate when he asked her to marry the family.

Her answer came nearly as quickly as the question had been posed. "Yes," she said. "I will."

Herman and Alice wrapped tails and plunged into the moon-lit water.

When the sun rose, Alice was the first to swim toward its light. Just as soon as she popped up above the water's surface, she dove back down. Her eyes widened, and she threw her fists in the air. A wedding gift from the sea wobbled along her new home's surface.

A fat Mottled Duck, perfect for Alice's first attempt at breakfast with her new family, quacked as it chewed on the morning's flies. The duck didn't seem very smart, which didn't surprise Alice since the feathered visitor was about fifteen miles from the closest marsh. Plus, when the water made a plopping sound from Alice's quick plunge back under, the duck just thought it had passed gas and went back to hunting.

But another hunter—one with more experience—was on a mission. Alice circled the rock. She became a shark, stalking an unsuspecting diver. A manatee, madly eyeing ripe algae.

Her hands inched closer and closer to the duck. Her arms reached further out of the water. She had her prey in sight—and within reach. Finally, she went in for what she knew would be her only chance at a quick kill.

As her body rose from the sea, her hands flung straight toward the duck's neck. When she had a good grip, she wrestled it to the top of the rock. Unfortunately for Alice, her new home was much closer to the sun than her last one, so it took three attempts to land her entire body on the rock. She was huffing, but she had breakfast.

The duck quacked feverishly, with its wings spread and ready for flight. But Alice had other plans for the unfortunate waterfowl. She lifted its body to her mouth and plunged her teeth into its delicate neck. It was impossible to tell where the blood began as Alice's crimson hair blew in the breeze.

When Olga and Elaine came to the surface, the duck was already plucked and ready to serve.

"Breakfast?" Olga asked.

"Yes," Alice replied. "I wanted to do something special."

"You are so thoughtful," Elaine said.

Alice handed the merwives their serving and began ravaging hers.

Olga rolled her shoulders and bit into her portion. "So gooooood!" she cried, licking her fingers after each bite. "Where's the rest of the breast? Seems mighty small for the rest of the lot to be this size."

Elaine huffed. "Don't you think we should wait for Herman and eat together? It's our first morning as a new family. And what's it matter to you, Olga? Alice prepared this for us as a treat. Just be appreciative."

"It's okay," Alice said timidly. "There—um—was a little otter nearby. He looked so pitiful. I couldn't say no."

"Hmm," Olga said.

Elaine looked over at Alice, but Alice whirled her head down quickly.

Olga turned back to her food and dangled the duck's liver above her mouth before she dropped it down her throat.

Elaine shook her head and nibbled slowly at her food.

⸺

The sun was nearing the center of the sky when Elaine finally finished her breakfast.

Alice rested flat against the top of her new home, taking in some of the day's hottest rays. "I can't believe Herman hasn't come up yet. The duck's probably already turned crispy," she said. She propped up and turned toward the other merwives. "Does he always sleep in like this?" she asked.

"Eh. I don't know. I try not to pay him any attention—haven't in decades," Olga said. She was sitting on the edge of the surface refereeing a wrestling match involving a romp of adolescent otters.

Elaine washed her hands of the duck's blood and sat beside Alice. "He's like many of the other mermen, you know. He swims with the kings—wants to be one of them." Elaine's voice changed. Yes, it was still friendly, but there was a firmness that didn't come naturally to her.

Elaine took Alice's hand and squeezed it. "We all have our secrets," she said.

"Yeah" Alice said, nodding.

Elaine leaned into Alice's hair, inching to her ear. "May I ask you a personal question?" she whispered.

"Anything," Alice said.

"Why didn't you stay with your pod after your husband died?"

"I didn't have a pod to stay with."

"What do you mean?"

"Rich wasn't like the kings, so he—we—didn't obey their laws. We believed the 'safety decree' was a lie just to make the kings happy."

"Oh. So why did you come here? Did Herman not tell you about us?"

"He did."

"So why then?"

"He seemed like he might be more like my Rich than maybe he wanted people to think. You know, the whole victim of circumstance thing. And then, last night felt so right. I felt like I belonged and that—well, I, I thought he—all of you—might be a role model and family for—never mind. I'm not making any sense."

"For whom, Alice? A family for whom?"

Alice turned her face toward the water. Her own secret wasn't entirely hers any longer. "For Ezra," she whispered. "My son."

"Your son? He's here. Out in the water? Isn't he?"

Alice nodded.

"I knew I heard him last night. And that's where the rest of the duck went, right?"

"Yes," Alice said.

"Does Herman know?"

"No," Alice replied. "Please don't hate me for not mentioning it before."

"I could never hate you."

The two mermaids fell back onto the rock.

Elaine reached for Alice's hand. "I don't mean to scare you," Elaine said. "But there is something you need to know about Herman. He's been getting closer with the kings. A lot closer. And the kings don't take kindly to merboys not of their own blood."

Alice didn't say a word. She couldn't. Instead, she squeezed Elaine's kind hand.

Thunder rattled Elaine from her sleep—well, that and Olga's ecstatic moaning. Olga sat with the fourth portion of duck and was devouring it.

"What?" she asked, noticing Elaine's eyes.

"That is for Herman."

"Whatever. He can come when the food is ready if he wants to eat it."

Elaine turned toward where Alice had been, but she was gone. "Where is Alice?" Elaine asked.

"She said she was going to find Herman before the storm comes in, but judging by that lightning over there, she doesn't have long to get back."

Just then, a screeching sound echoed across the sea.

"Eeeee! Eeeee! Eeeee!"

Elaine slithered to the edge and peered out at the sea. "What is that?"

"Eeeee! Eeeee! Eeeee!"

Olga licked her fingers. "It's those idiot dolphins. They are probably in heat."

"No. They. Are. Not," Elaine said, recognizing the voice. Before she said another word, she plunged into the water.

The lightning moved closer to their home.

Olga washed her hands and moved to the side of rock that Elaine had just dived from. "Don't electrocute yourself, you old fool!" Olga shouted.

Elaine's orange head popped out of the dirty water, searching the rolling sea. A starfish stuck to the side of her face. The clouds lowered, and flashes of light shot around her. The water roared—covering her. She fought until she was breathing air again.

"Get back to this rock, Elaine! It's not safe out there," Olga said.

Elaine turned back. "It's Alice!" she called, pointing toward the bobbing crimson dot on the horizon. "Something has her! Or her merchild!"

"A merchild! We have a merchild and nobody told me about it?!" Olga shouted, following Elaine into the sea.

Sand washed into their eyes, and the upset water spit them out over and over again. But, still, they swam.

"Eeeee! Eeeee! Eeeee!" Alice cried. "Eeeee! Eeeee! Eeeee!"

Elaine reached Alice first, but the youngest merwife only whispered something unintelligible. Elaine grabbed Alice's arm and yanked her back toward home.

Alice resisted the pull, fighting to go back deeper into the water. Whispering again.

Olga reached Elaine and Alice as the young mermaid continued to pull into the angry sea. "She's bleeding," Olga said, grabbing Alice's arm.

Elaine let go of Alice to try and inspect her better. Crimson stains covered her body. "Alice, where are you hurt?"

Alice's ignored Elaine's question. She mumbled again, pointing to the waters below. The waves and thunder canceled all of her sounds.

Olga dived below and checked Alice's torso and tail. Finally, she found it. She came up to the surface and told Elaine they needed to unclench Alice's fist. "She has a death grip on it. And whatever it is, it's sharp. It cut me, and I barely brushed the tip of it," Olga said.

"Let's get her home first," Elaine said. "She needs to be home."

Olga didn't argue. She didn't have time to. She picked up Alice and put her on Elaine's back. "Go," she said. "I'll see if I can find the merchild."

Elaine hugged Olga. "His name is Ezra," she said. Then, she swam away.
"Ezra!"

"Ezra!"

"Ezra!" Olga called, holding her hands to her lips and yelling as loudly as she had ever yelled.

She waited and listened, but, with the storm, she couldn't make out anything. When Olga flicked her tail to propel her search, she immediately crashed into the merboy. Even in his unconscious state, he obeyed her. Olga liked him even without him having to try.

Although his body failed to penetrate the surface, his deep, bright eyes shone through the sea's reflective glaze. He was half the size of Alice, and he, like Alice, possessed a wild crimson crown. "Up you go," Olga whispered to the merboy, draping him over her shoulders.

"Can you carry him?" Elaine asked, calling back from up ahead.

"Don't worry about me. Now swim on back home, and don't make me pass you."

At home on the rock, the sea still raged.

Alice rolled atop the rock and saw Ezra. The lightning show didn't even tempt her. Her eyes went directly to the merboy's chest, and she watched as it rose and fell. She nearly cried, but, instead, a cough sputtered from her lips. Her voice was coming back—slowly. "Her-er-er," she whispered. "Her-er-er," she tried again.

"Hermit crab?" Olga guessed, holding Alice's hand.

Alice shook her head. "Her-er-er," she tried again.

"Herman?" Elaine asked. "Herman?"

"We don't know where he is. Hardly ever do," Olga added. "Wish I never did."

Elaine swatted at Olga. "Now is not the time for your mess, Olga."

"Herman," Alice said, reverting the attention back to herself. She extended her clutched hand to her merwives. Elaine and Olga, so wrapped up in getting Alice and Ezra to safety, had forgotten about the sharp object that slit the soft skin of Alice's hand.

When Alice opened her fist and dropped the item, Elaine and Olga gasped and leapt from Alice's side as they both splashed into the water. Slowly, though, they came back to the rock—and to Alice.

They peeked at what the youngest mermaid's hand had held and soon found themselves entranced.

"It's his fluke," Elaine whispered, poking it.

Perfectly turquoise. Glittering even under the clouds.

"Yeah, shriveled and all wrinkly. It's his for sure," Olga added.

"Please," Elaine said, putting her hands in the air and breathing a deep sigh.

Alice drifted back off to sleep. Elaine swatted her tail from one side of the rock to the other, and she rubbed her hands together as if she were trying to start a fire.

Olga took Herman's fluke and tossed it into the sea.

"What are you doing?" Elaine shouted.

"If the otters are going to compete in any serious wrestling matches, they need to put on some weight," Olga said.

Elaine began to cry.

Olga went to her dearest friend in the world and wrapped her arms around Elaine's neck. "We will be okay," Olga said. "I promise."

Elaine and Olga, after a good rest, emerged from the nighttime waters to find, miraculously, that their latest two pod members were back to normal.

Alice, with a feathery bandage wrapped around her hand, finished the preparations on another duck, and Ezra questioned the otters about a wrestling league for merboys.

"He found Ezra and tried to kill him, didn't he?" Elaine asked, sitting beside Alice.

"He did," Alice replied.

"And you killed him first?"

"I did."

Elaine was quiet for a moment as she shook her head. "I tried to see the best even when there wasn't a best to see. But Olga was right. He was a selfish, cruel merman. Always wanted to be a king and would get rid of anyone or anything in his way."

Alice put down the duck and looked at Elaine. "We will leave if you'd like. I didn't mean for any of this to happen."

"Nonsense," Olga said, plopping down between the two mermaids. "It would've been us in his way in a matter of time. All it would've taken is one king giving the order. Now hush up about him. We have a merboy to raise."

Ezra came quickly from the edge and sat beside Alice. "Good morning, Miss Olga and Miss Elaine. I hope you like duck. I killed it this morning."

"A merboy with manners and willing to work around this rock," Olga said, reaching around and patting Ezra's back. "Color me impressed."

Elaine took a moment and looked among the members of her merpod. Everyone was smiling; everyone was laughing. There was love. For the first time since she was a mergirl, she felt like things were truly right. "Welcome to the pod," she said.

Together, as a family, they devoured another stupid, stupid duck.

# THE TRAPPER

**THE WOMAN'S VOICE QUIVERS AS** she stutters into the receiver. The static haunting the line masks most of her fear even if she doesn't know it. "T-t-this is Marie," she says. "Is this the trapper?" she asks. Chase's voice breaks too as he assures her that he is the one she seeks even if he doesn't call himself "the trapper." They've been in touch for weeks now. He is slow to answer her remaining questions. He asks few of his own. His voice is low. And timid. His eyes close as he converses with her, listening for the voice of his father to find him.

But Marie interrupts his concentration. She's precise, giving Chase directions to her home. At first, he only nods to himself, careful not to be too eager, but when she repeats herself, he realizes he must speak. "Yes," he says quietly. "I'll be there soon."

*"It's time," the father says to the mother. "Will you get him?"*

*With both of her hands, she cups his face and leans down slowly to kiss his forehead.*

*"He will have to do it alone," he whispers into her ear.*

*She nods. Then, she leaves to bring in their son.*

*In only a few seconds, the son, Chase, enters the room and takes the father's hand into his own. Chase knows what this man before him is. And, consequently, he knows what he is—and will always be. What he's unsure of is if they are gifts or curses.*

---

When Chase arrives at the house, candlelight highlights the silhouetted moving bodies inside. He watches briefly and is careful when he finally knocks. He remembers his training.

When the knob turns, he steps back. A woman with dark, fading hair answers. "Hello," she whispers. Her eyes are swollen and damp. It's the woman from the phone—he has no doubt. "Marie," Chase says. "I'm here for the traveler." He fumbles with his bag so it rests in the crevice of his elbow, and he extends his hand. She nods and accepts his kindness. She doesn't let go; instead, she pulls him inside. As she releases him, her fingers brush against his bag. He can tell her touch wasn't unintentional.

A breeze sweeps against Chase's ankles. He steps back and closes the door. He'd forgotten. So had Marie. But she's already gone ahead, back among the others.

Chase crosses the narrow hallway and stands in the back of the cold room, where he observes the traveler's visitors. They move to the traveler and take the man's hands and squeeze them against their own bodies. They whisper into his ears and step away. Marie remains at the traveler's bedside. She's waiting; she isn't living.

She glances at Chase to make sure he's near. Her monitoring of the invited trapper increases as the night wears on.

Even the traveler knows—or at least he did—that Chase is here to trap. He's the one who signed the form when Chase's father was the one doing the trapping.

The traveler's visitors look at Chase. The trapper knows what's behind their eyes. He sees it himself in his own reflection. His hand twitches, but he clenches his fist. He listens for his father's voice.

They want a trapper. He reminds himself of this.

When the first rattle begins, Chase shuffles and clutches his bag. First it's one tear, and then there are more. A storm of them, splattering against the floor. Breaths collapse. The traveler shakes.

Chase approaches the bed. He whispers into Marie's ear. "Two may stay," he says. This number is the maximum his father implemented. He was firm on this stipulation.

Marie stands and kisses the traveler's cheek. Then she steps to the side of the bed and puts her arm around a young woman, whose eyes remind Chase of Marie's. But also of the traveler's. They are a part of her. Marie cups her hand around the woman's ear and leans into her. The woman nods, and the two hopeful souls hold hands as they approach the traveler.

Chase puts his bag on the foot of the bed and unbuttons the flap. He slowly winds the zipper down to the end of the bag.

"Stay away from his exits," Chase says. "Head. Toes. Chest."

Marie and the young woman stand near the traveler's waist. Huddled. They both cling to the man's hand.

"It will be soon," Chase adds.

The young woman clears her throat. Marie puts her hand to her forehead and nods. Then, they both turn, and they look pleadingly into Chase's eyes. He's careful not to look away too quickly.

He reaches into his bag and retrieves the dove-feathered net.

Once it's in his arms, he unfolds it and holds it against the light. His eyes inspect each inch.

"It's time to back away from him," Chase says.

They obey. They say nothing to the traveler. They forget there is a present. Why even have it when the future is all that is desired?

Chase is slow as he tucks the edges of the net around the traveler. Quietly, he unrolls the tape and secures the traveler's encasing. Then, he waits. So does the family. They've had so much practice that it's almost welcome.

*The father's never been a man of extravagances. Even now, he saves his breaths for when the time comes. And it's near. They both know this. "I know I can do it. I had the best teacher, Dad," Chase says as he reaches for the satchel his father keeps under his bed.*

*It's with this movement that Chase's father opens his eyes.*

*"Leave it be. I told you. I want to go where they used to go."*

———

The net stirs as the exit begins. Chase tells the family to relax, but he is ready to leap if a corner comes undone. He stands on the tips of his toes and watches the corners of the net. One end jumps, and soon another joins it. Then, the traveler becomes frantic. Corners fly. Feathers stretch. It looks as though the traveler might take flight.

Chase assures the family that what is happening is normal. This isn't entirely true because there is no normal.

He thinks of offering them something else. But this is their peace. This is their choice.

Rest suddenly finds the traveler.

Chase asks Marie and the young woman to leave the room so he can collect the traveler's spirit for them.

Their faces tell him they want to object, but he explains that it's necessary for a successful trapping.

"Fine," Marie says. She grabs the other woman's hand again, and they leave the room, not looking back as they go.

———

*"I'm scared," Chase admits.*

*"We all are. Of something," his father says.*

*"But I'll miss you."*

*"And I you."*

*"Can't I keep you?"*

*"Close your eyes, Chase."*

*"Okay."*

*"Close them tight."*

*"I am."*

*"Now, listen."*

*"I don't hear anything."*

*"Listen harder."*

*"There's nothing, Dad."*

*"Chase, you have to want to hear it."*

*"What am I listening for?"*

*"For me. It's how you'll keep me."*

*"But I can trap you."*

*"I don't want to be trapped."*

*"But we are trappers, Dad."*

*"We don't always choose what we are."*

*"But I want you with me for always."*

*"I will be."*

*"Where will you be then?"*

*"Close your eyes. Do you hear anything?"*

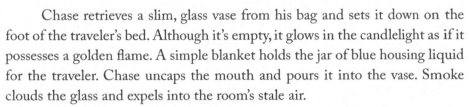

Chase retrieves a slim, glass vase from his bag and sets it down on the foot of the traveler's bed. Although it's empty, it glows in the candlelight as if it possesses a golden flame. A simple blanket holds the jar of blue housing liquid for the traveler. Chase uncaps the mouth and pours it into the vase. Smoke clouds the glass and expels into the room's stale air.

He takes this new vessel to the head of the traveler, where he guides the opening to the edge of the net and begins to loosen the tape.

The first taste of warmth hits Chase's fingers, and he angles the opening and waits for the splash. It comes in only a second.

When he seals the jar, he calls her. "Marie," he says. But he realizes she's behind a door. "Marie!" he calls louder. He goes to the door and opens it.

The same eyes that had watched the trapper from the back of the room now stand in front of him, and they are changed, looking now at the boy.

"Marie," he says softly. "I trapped him."

The woman's mouth opens and she cries. "Are you sure?" asks the young woman who'd remained by the traveler's bedside.

"I am," Chase replies.

He unveils the shimmering vase and hands it to Marie.

She takes the vase and collapses to her knees.

The others gather around her and admire the burning glass vessel.

Chase turns around and goes back into the room to collect his bag. When he returns, Marie and the others are on the floor.

"Griff," Marie says. "Tell us you are okay."

A man's voice begins to mumble from under the closed lid.

Chase wants to ask Marie if the traveler sounds like she remembers him. He wants to know if he's the same. If he's happy again. If he wishes he could've gone where the others go. But Chase doesn't say a word. Instead, the trapper walks out into the darkness and begins his journey home. He doesn't have a glowing vessel to light his path. He has something else. He has his father's voice. In his memories. In his heart. In his world.

# IN THE HOLLOW

**I**N AN OVERGROWN FIELD FLOODED with nutsedge and white clover, Walt gripped the rock that proclaimed the memory of her name. Tears streamed down his rosy cheeks. "With Momma here, it's hallowed ground," he said. "They taught us in class that it's a sin to leave hallowed ground, Pa! A punishing sin!"

Joseph, who stood over his son, bent and pried the boy's hands loose from the snaggy edges of the flat, oddly-shaped stone. "I've done said we're leaving," he said.

It didn't take but a second for Joseph to get a sturdy grip on his boy, and when he did, he dragged Walt from her grave.

Walt was no longer crying. Instead, he was begging for forgiveness.

Joseph didn't even look back.

———

It was a few counties over where Joseph, by himself, built the three-room cabin in the spot of the hollow that the sun refused to touch. It was a land that offered pine trees as towering gods and tenebrous caves as entrances into unknown worlds. It birthed winds whose whispers contained secrets just as assuredly as its creeks sang mysterious melodies.

Once the home stood, he turned his attention to the untamed fields. Joseph worked to unearth the hearts of rotten stumps and to clear the damp leaves.

Within a handful of months, darkness spread deeper into the hollow, suffocating the land. In a matter of days, stalks retreated into the very soil from which they'd sprung. Seeds soon skipped entire lifetimes in favor of remaining in their earthly cocoons.

Crickets abandoned their music, and the bullfrogs' deep-throated warbles faded into silence.

The branches from the pines ceased dancing altogether. The wind, no matter how much it insisted, couldn't persuade them otherwise. Being still could make them seem unnoticed—for a while.

"It's a sign from Momma that we need to go back," said Walt, who had been sick since the move and unable to join his father on the porch most evenings.

"Ain't no such thing as *a sign*," Joseph replied without looking at his son.

"But what if it is?"

"This here is our home," Joseph said. He stood and gripped Walt's shoulder before he let go and went inside.

Alone, a sharp, scratching sound caught Walt's attention. The boy stood and walked to the edge of the porch, where he looked toward town only a half-hour walk away. A celebration of some kind, perhaps. But when the noise came again, louder, he realized the sound was from inside the hollow.

He didn't sit back down. Instead, he too stepped inside the cabin.

As he shut the door, he told himself it was only the static from his father's radio.

By the end of the season, Walt wasn't able to get out of his bed for more than a few minutes at a time. At first, trips outside were once—maybe twice—a week. After a few weeks, fortuitous nighttime journeys for the boy were no more. Drinks of water could wait as could trips to the bathroom. Only the light from the flickering flames of the kerosene lamps strayed from beneath his bedroom door once the moon appeared.

Nighttime dustings of snow painted the still-darkening landscape. Walt prayed to his mother, asking her to send more if she could—to hide the other things that began to appear inside the snowfall.

For the first few sightings, he blamed his dreams. It was only after he worked up the strength to examine the jagged cuts along the outside of his window one morning that he could no longer deny the proof. Soft, blonde chunks of fur lay atop the melting snow.

Joseph, even with the evidence Walt brought him, denied what existed inside the hollow. "This here is our home," he said again and again.

When Angus, Joseph's brother, visited from the city after the first big snow of winter melted, only Joseph was well enough to greet the visitor at the train station along the edge of town.

As the brothers strolled down the empty streets of town, Joseph pointed to the country store he frequently visited and told stories about the different kinds of seeds he'd purchased there. Angus, a staunch advocate of formality and public reputation, interrupted his brother's small talk to scold him for coming to the train station in attire that wasn't even as nice as Angus's Sunday worst. It was a typical conversation for a relationship such as theirs.

Once they stepped foot under the pines of the hollow, Joseph stopped to light the kerosene lantern he held under his arms. "We need help just to get to your home?" Angus asked, knowing better than to expect a response.

The men arrived at the front porch and made use of the rocking chairs. Angus's voice sank to a lower timbre. "There's a brooding darkness among this land," he said. "A lantern just to see. There aren't even any animals moving amidst the brush. Surely you find those things odd, Brother?"

"It gets dark early in winter. Animals hibernate."

"I don't think what you have here is a symptom of the season. Don't you find the prolonged ill state of your boy peculiar?"

"You and me both know I've seen the horrors influenza can do. It ain't supernatural. Now, Walt's gonna be fine," Joseph replied.

"You said in your written correspondence that Walt's been sick since you got here."

"If by *written correspondence* you mean my letters, I don't think that's true," Joseph said.

Angus rolled his shoulders. "As you believe then. But, in the very least, you would think you would've learned to listen," he added.

Joseph stared into Angus's eyes. "What did you say?"

"You left hallowed land, Joseph," Angus said.

Joseph was already up from his rocker, the sole of his shoe propping open the front door. "Forgive me. It's been a long trip," Angus said, stepping inside.

Joseph ignored Angus and led him down the hallway and to the guest bedroom. "We'll all catch up in the morning. I'm sure Walt will feel better after a night's rest and can join us," Joseph said, standing crookedly in the frame. Angus grabbed the knob and began to bring the door to, but Joseph caught it with his hand. "Room's got a lamp. Enough kerosene for the night," he said.

Although the two brothers had been gone from the other's side for nearly a decade, they both recognized what the other was thinking.

———————

At morning, Joseph knocked on Angus's bedroom door. Nothing inside stirred, so Joseph tapped again. After another failed attempt to awaken anything within, Joseph turned the knob and peeked inside. The covers on the bed were pulled tight, and the pillow was without a dent. The only change from before Angus's arrival was the addition of a piece of paper propped against the side of the burning lamp that rested on the nightstand under the room's lone window.

Joseph shuffled into the room and retrieved the curious object. Upon inspection, Joseph prodded in his shirt's pocket for his pair of thin-rimmed spectacles and quickly fixed them onto the tip of his nose. He held each word the letter contained:

*Dear Brother,*

*I thank you for such gracious hospitality during my short stay, but I fear it is in my best interest to return home at once. Father and Mother raised us in a way that condemned unnecessary fictions, so please know my sincerity in authoring these words. I don't know how to write what I feel I must say in any kind of delicate fashion, so I will speak with truth as best I know it. In this hollow, there is beyond a mere darkness that I hinted at upon my arrival. I see the queer stances of the trees and the shadows that dance upon your walls. Although I doubted my eyes at first, I saw something outside, stalking my window. I felt the eyes upon me, inspecting my person. I will not describe it in detail because I do not wish to ever recall what it is I saw. You must recognize that there is something evil brooding inside the silence of your hollow. I sense you know what I speak of and hope you will evacuate the home you so adore. I beg you to return to your land—your home—before it is too late.*

*With Sincerity,*
*Angus P. Williams*

Joseph tore through the house and ripped the letter into pieces, tossing the remains into the living room's blazing hearth.

As he watched his brother's words burn, a tug on his sleeve pulled his attention away from the flames. "Uncle Angus is already gone," Walt said. "Left as soon as morning arrived and he could make out the path. I gave him one of our lanterns to help."

"It's good to see you out of the bed," Joseph said, patting his son on the back.

"I thought he was going to help you gather more wood for winter?" Walt said.

"Left a note saying he had other things on his mind. Wouldn't be much help."

"He was scared," Walt said, pulling up a chair to the fire. "He told me so. I think he saw one of them."

"There ain't nothing to see, Walt. Except some snow," Joseph said. "Anyhow, are you feeling better?"

"I don't imagine that I ever will," he said, leaving his chair where it sat and returning to his bedroom.

According to the voice on the radio, what would likely be the biggest snow of the season was on its way early, and Joseph left Walt alone inside for the morning while he went into the woods to cut logs for the fire.

At first, Joseph traveled deep in the hollow with a flashlight attached to his cap and his sharpened ax in his hand, but when the first tree fell without any of its dry leaves rustling as they tumbled down against the ground, he returned to the outer edge, a place where, if the light was positioned right, he could keep his home within sight. Still, even there, not a single hungry bird cawed. No stray moles pattered. Nothing. The only noise that came when the giant trees fell was a thud against the frozen ground, but even that was more of a feeling than a sound.

After Joseph had a handful of trees down, a dark, heavy silhouette of a man, set apart from the haunting blackness of the hollow by its own unnatural light, stole his attention. The figure moved along the edge of the yard. Joseph held his ax tight against his chest and ran.

"Hello?" Joseph called to the figure. "Who is it?" he repeated louder, angrier. But no voice replied.

When Joseph reached the unanticipated visitor, he recognized the old man as the stocker at the country store up the road.

The old man didn't bother extending his hand. He stood with his arms crossed against his denim coat as his burning lantern dangled from the cup of his palm.

"I'd offer you some coffee, but Walt is sick," Joseph said.

The man faced the ground as he spoke. "I imagine so. The first snow has come."

"Excuse me?" Joseph asked.

"Your boy will only get worse."

"He's feeling some better actually. He got out of bed this morning."

The old man spit on the ground. "I'm not here to argue. Figured I'd give you the respect of letting you know to watch your boy. That's why I'm here. If he's the sick one, it's him they're after."

"They who?"

The old man finally looked up at Joseph. "The ones who are the keepers of hallowed land. Call them what you want."

Joseph laughed. "And how do you know my story?"

"Everybody in town knows everybody else's story," the man said.

"I see," Joseph said quietly. "Anyways, ain't no such thing as 'keepers of hallowed land.' I ain't a superstitious man. Never been one."

"Then why does sickness surround you? Look at you. Sick land. Sick boy. Hell, it ain't even me that broke the oath to the land, and I can hear them among us."

"I don't hear anything," Joseph said.

"Exactly," the old man said. "Silence. When they come, they bring silence with them."

Joseph folded his arms and looked among the trees. "Who is with you?" Joseph asked, losing a stray, white shadow behind one of the pines.

The old man huffed and headed back toward the road. He glanced once more at Joseph and spoke, but Joseph couldn't hear a word.

Instead of finishing up the wood, Joseph went inside to check on Walt. The boy was in his bed, turned toward the window. He'd brought another lantern into his room. Still, even together, the flickering flames struggled to keep the boy's space lit. A quilt his mother had made hugged his body. He didn't face his father when the man entered the room although Walt knew it was him.

"I told you we should've never left. We're damned sinners, Pa," Walt said.

"You ain't a sinner, Walt. You are a boy," Joseph explained, sitting on the edge of Walt's bed.

"Momma was there. We were supposed to stay."

"Your mother's gone on. It's only me and you. You know that."

"You don't leave hallowed ground, Pa, and we did."

"You should give it a chance here. The land might grow on you."

"It's too late now," Walt said, and he pointed toward the window.

"Too late for wha—look at that," Joseph said.

The man got up and went to the window, where he watched the densest snow he'd ever seen begin to illuminate the sky as if the milky flakes were of holy descent.

Walt took the quilt and pulled it over his head. "You don't hear it, do you?" he asked.

"You can't hear anything in the snow," Joseph said, staring outside. "I guess I better go get some more wood for fire while I still can. We don't want the one going to get snuffed out."

Joseph walked back over to Walt's bed and tousled his son's hair. Then, he left.

Finally alone, Walt uncovered himself and went to the window and waited. It didn't take long. When the first paw pressed against the glass, he unlatched the lock and welcomed them inside.

Joseph didn't bother flipping the light on his cap back on. The brightness of the snow was enough. He ran to the shed and upended the overturned wheelbarrow. The tire was nearly flat, but it worked well enough as he guided it over the smooth snowy ground toward the few pieces of firewood he'd managed to cut earlier.

He dusted each stick before he dumped it into the aluminum carrier, but by the time the next piece was ready to be added to the pile, snow already covered it again.

With the snow falling, the hollow was quieter—if that was possible. No crunching of frozen leaves when he walked. When the sticks smacked against the sides of the wheelbarrow, nothing came from it. His hard breaths lost themselves somehow before they could reach his ears.

Joseph tucked his head low between his shoulders and, driving the wheelbarrow, followed his fading footprints back to the cabin.

With an armful of wood, Joseph entered the house. The quiet followed him inside. He opened his mouth to call his son to help him set the wood for the fire, but, although his lips moved, nothing came. He tried again, but, still, the sound failed him.

He bobbled the chopped logs. A few crashed to the floor. He stumbled over them. Amidst it all, silence met him.

He turned to the light of the fire to help him gather what he'd dropped, but the flame sputtered and died. When it was extinguished so, too, was the light from the snow.

The shadow covered him. All of him and everything he knew inside the shadowed hollow.

In the darkness, he felt for the table where one of the lanterns rested. When he had it in his arms, he ripped off the cover and fumbled with the matches. Each strike blank.

Joseph tried to call his son again. His mouth formed the words, but, still, nothing came from within him. He fell to the ground and beat on the floor. The pine, though, gave him nothing in return.

But then a sound came. Walt's bedroom door creaked open, the rusty hinges showing life. And there was light. Finally, finally light. Moving closer and closer.

Joseph began to stand, ready to embrace his son—ready to take his boy into his arms.

As soon as Joseph found his footing, he collapsed again.

In a single-file line, erect and resigned, the fantastic family came parading down the hallway. Their bodies coated with white and glowing fur. Their heads ripping the hanging boards from the ceiling. Snouts covering the tips of fangs that dipped below blackened smiles. Paws with splintered nails beat against their sides. There were six. Seven. Nine. Twelve. Joseph tried to count, but he lost track as they circled him.

He attempted to say his boy's name. "Wal-wal-wal-wal-wal-"

"Walt!" It finally came.

"Walt!"

"Walt!"

He yelled it until he could yell no more. The name echoed throughout the algid cabin. The creatures stood and listened, themselves frozen and quiet.

Then, Walt's door creaked again, and the boy emerged holding a lantern.

The beasts made room for him to join his father.

Walt joined the man on the floor as he sat on his knees and put his hand to his father's ear. "They know Momma," the boy whispered.

Tears streamed down Joseph's face. "I know you miss her. I miss her, too," he said.

"But I'm going to see her," Walt said, smiling.

"No. No. Not for many, many years," Joseph said, his tears cutting at each word.

"Now, Pa. They forgive me. They forgive me!" Walt said.

Joseph began to embrace his son, but the white, glowing paws took the boy away.

Joseph tried to pull him back—to take his son and to leave, to return to the place where the boy had been well and where they'd known trust and comfort and love. But it was too late.

Surrounded by the numbing silence, they, the beasts Joseph did not believe in, with their furiously blazing white light, were upon the unsullied boy.

# THE HUNT

## I

**I**T WASN'T THAT LONG AGO that Zoey had sat at her kitchen-table desk. It was absent of framed photos, personalized coasters, or anything else she found to be essentially useless. Rather, she used her space to house those objects she relied on over and over again: her wooden yardstick, her fine-point black pen, her tape dispenser, and her countless reams of recycled printer paper.

After she performed her creative magic with her tools and had the specs just right, she meticulously taped the edges of each new sheet onto her ongoing project so that what she looked at possessed the illusion of not even really being cheap, patched-together paper at all. It became, instead, a thin, unrecognizably homemade scroll of a map, and it reached so far down when it was open that it brushed against the eternally-crispy, ketchup-stained relics of potato cakes that ruined the room's rug.

Zoey did keep one part-time decorative item near her desk. With a piece of twine wrapped around the plastic loop at its base, her flashlight dangled against the back of her chair, clinking the dinged wood each time the AC kicked on. The music of her dancing flashlight fueled her adrenaline—the adrenaline she needed to keep up if her map was to lead her to the mysterious sasquatch that she so believed was out *there*.

Her earliest memories were of the elusive creature. Not the real one, of course, but of the fictional protagonist from *The Sasquatch in the Woods*.

On one of their first mother-daughter outings after the big move from the city earlier in the summer, Cheryl took Zoey to Creekmore's small library. It was certainly different from the main branch in St. Louis—the one at which Cheryl and Eric had both worked through college and had recently left for teaching positions at the expanding community college a couple of hours away. Creekmore's library was about the size of one half of one floor of the St. Louis location, but it still contained the same sense of magic that Zoey found familiar.

In its lonely aisles, she sat on the carpeted floor and traced her fingertips along the faded books' spines until she came to *The Sasquatch in the Woods*.

When she got to her room and curled into the comfort of her cool bedsheets, she fell into the story as her mother read from the whimsically illustrated pages.

On their next trip to the library, Zoey scanned the covers as she had before but she didn't reach for anything in particular. Cheryl picked a handful of titles she thought would work and, with Zoey at her side, headed to the checkout desk. As Cheryl talked with the part-time helper, Zoey walked over to the cart where she and her mother had returned the previous book, and she grabbed it again. She took it to Cheryl and poked her in the hip with its blunted edge. "This one," she said. Cheryl laughed and put it on the counter.

Each time they returned to the library, Zoey asked to recheck the book—until she could make out all the words herself.

It was impossible to know what exactly it was about the story that struck the toddler, but it consumed her imagination. And her life.

Sasquatch-printed socks. Sasquatch-shaped cookies. Sasquatch Halloween costumes. It became all things sasquatch all the time.

In the years that followed, Zoey and her mother, with the help of the patient librarian, explored every word that the shelves (and back room and computer) contained about the sasquatch.

Once there were no other stories or articles left to read, Zoey's parents thought their daughter might move on—that maybe her preoccupation had been only an eccentric phase in her development.

They believed that was the case, but one evening Eric stepped into Zoey's bedroom closet to put away a freshly laundered quilt and saw something that let him know they were wrong.

On the white wall, drawn with a mixture of markers, chalk, and crayons, were the places Zoey and her family had hiked inside Wonder Rock, the nearby state park, on recent weekends, and the "X"s marked the places where the sasquatch was not.

"I'm getting closer," Zoey said to her father as they both gazed at her map. "I know I am."

On most evenings when dinner arrived at her desk, Zoey took her plate and placed it on the floor. In her unofficial uniform of an untucked crimson-checkered flannel shirt, a gold sasquatch pin, and a pair of faded jeans, she measured and drew until long after her food was cold and stale. Occasionally, when her parents reminded her of what she was missing, she stuck her finger down into the separate pools of cold mush and brought back a taste, but those morsels were all she needed. Her true nourishment came from the hope of the unmet promises her map contained.

With her map already sprawling with the detailed curvatures and intricacies of Wonder Rock's caves, streams, stumps, and ponds, Zoey flawlessly sketched the images of their weekend world with names that made it even more personal—more theirs.

The cave with the black, slimy bottom was "Zoey's Dinky Dungeon." She laughed when her dad suggested it, and she traced the name elegantly across the top of the cave.

The first cave they'd visited almost two years ago after the reveal of Zoey's closet drawing—and, consequently, the one when their "hikes" became "hunts"—had golden walls that looked as though an artist had taken to the cold, damp insides with a can of glittery spray paint. It was coined "Zoey's Palace." Cheryl kissed her daughter's cheek after Zoey suggested the name.

There was "Zoey's Mysterious Rock," "Zoey's Glowing Vessel," and "Zoey's Eerie Darkness" for a few of the other caves, but there was also "Cheryl's Seat" for a huge stump the entire family usually squatted on for a quick rest before heading too deep into the woods to follow whatever path might be next.

When Zoey asked what she should label her favorite rivulet, the one where she pointed out what she had sworn were *almost*-washed-away footprints, Cheryl quickly shouted, "Eric's Babbling Brook!"

Eric, as if he'd been awaiting the cue, turned his mouth toward the ceiling and gurgled a noise that somehow mimicked the water's peaceful sound. Cheryl tried to join in, but the first note of her attempt sparked a coughing fit.

As Cheryl and Eric fell into one another laughing, Zoey touched up her map.

## ||

**O**N THE LAST SATURDAY OF October, which also happened to be Zoey's tenth birthday, the family was out and hunting before the sun had had the time to reach the horizon.

Zoey considered the hunt a birthday miracle in itself. With the heavy rain from the day (and night) before, she knew she might have to miss out on an adventure and settle for cake and ice cream from the local Cheapies with the usual company of her parents. Not that that would be so bad. Over breakfast, they'd asked if she had any friends she wanted to invite over, and when she didn't answer, they'd dropped the subject more quickly than usual.

Cheryl and Eric would surprise Zoey with a couple of gifts she didn't know she wanted, sing to her at the top of every hour, and watch a movie of her choosing that night on the couch. It would be a good day and she'd be happy. The next morning things would be back to normal with no memories of a found sasquatch.

But since Zoey was still Zoey—and couldn't take any chances of missing a minute of sasquatch hunting—she slept in her button-up shirt and jeans just in case. When Cheryl and Eric shook her awake as the clear moonlight sneaked through her blinds, she only had to secure her pin to her shirt's pocket before she was ready to go.

As she and her parents sat down at Cheryl's Stump for sugary granola bars and hot chocolate, Zoey reached into the inside pocket of her denim jacket and pulled out her map. She fumbled with her flashlight as she tried to balance the two items. Her mother helped by grabbing the rolled map and delicately gliding off the hair tie that held it so perfectly.

Cheryl unspooled the map and gave one end to Eric, and they held it above the prickly bushes and mud-caked, damp leaves. "Okay, Zoey," she said. "Which cave is it?"

"Hmm…" Zoey hummed.

Cheryl, looking at her daughter, slowly uttered, "If you were a sasquatch, where would you be?"

Her questioning only made Zoey more eager, and she moved from one side of her mother to the other, squeezing between her parents. Then she pointed her flashlight toward her map and guided the bright, white light up and down the inked routes.

Eric's index finger traced behind the glow, helping zero in on the cave she might select.

"How about up here?" Zoey asked as she pointed to a path that led to a cave not far away.

"Hey, I remember seeing that cave," Eric said. Noticing how focused his daughter was at selecting the right one—*the one*—he wrapped his arm around her shoulders. "Your mom and I are good with whichever one you choose. Honey, you know the sasquatch isn't—"

"Stop!" Zoey interrupted. "Don't say it." She pushed his arm away.

"Zoey," Cheryl said, getting her daughter's attention back to the map. "Is this cave the one?"

Cheryl looked up at Eric and rolled her shoulders as Zoey considered the question.

When the image of the tracks reentered her mind, she broke her stock-still stance and quickly put her hair in a ponytail with the tie that had kept her map tightly wound. "That's the cave," she said.

With the sun finally peeking through the tops of the trees, Zoey shoved her flashlight in her back pocket, and after one quick glance at her map to get her bearings, she took off running up the trail. She turned back to her parents when she had a good lead. "Last one there's a sasquatchless loser," she said.

"Be careful!" her parents shouted.

The two adults shared a quick glance. "Do you think we are doing the right thing?" Cheryl asked.

"I don't know. I thought she would've grown out of this whole sasquatch thing by now," Eric said. "Do you know why she wants to believe in it so much?"

"No."

Lost, they finished rolling the map.

---

Cheryl and Eric caught up with their daughter when they stepped into the shadow of the cave's stone confines and found her slamming her muddy boots against the wall. Marble-sized clods danced about before they rolled into the awaiting darkness.

"Lightening the load," Zoey explained upon seeing her parents. She gave her boots one last good smack and pulled them on.

Cheryl sat on the hard slab and loosened her backpack strap. When her bag was beside her, she undid the zipper and retrieved a bottle of water, taking a couple of swigs. She passed it to Eric, who was leaning against the freshly mud-coated wall and wiping his face with a sweat-stained bandana. "Any sasquatch that might've been in here escaped through the back with all the racket you were making," he said.

"I'm not far enough inside for the sound to travel all the way back *there*," Zoey said, extending her arm as far as she could and pointing.

She shook her head and walked over to her mother. "Did you see the sasquatch's tracks?"

"I saw some tracks."

"They lead to the cave, you know."

Cheryl stood and wrapped her arms around her daughter. "I hope so, sweetie," she said.

"Come on," Zoey said, switching on her flashlight and leading her family into the darkness.

---

When the glow of the natural world was a thing of the past, Cheryl and Eric pulled out their own sources of battery-powered light and joined theirs with Zoey's.

Slowly, they continued on their hunt as they carefully navigated around boulders and wedged between jagged crevices.

The floor gave them the unfortunate gift of suction, and droplets of water began to splash each time they lifted their feet.

They moved more quickly toward the back of the cave—so far that the water soon rose to their shins and pulled them along.

They hobbled as they tried to retain their balance. Mother, father, and daughter looked as if they were a family of tightrope walkers, with their quivering arms outstretched and their wobbling legs barely keeping them upright. Instead of strong gusts of air to knock them off their perch, it was stray waves they had to navigate.

No matter how carefully they moved, water still spilled over the tops of their boots, and ripples splashed against their waists.

"Don't fall, Eric!" Cheryl loudly instructed over the sloshing water.

"Ha ha, Mom," Zoey said, knowing for whom the message was really intended. "He won't. He's being careful."

"Yeah he is," Eric added.

"Good. Just keep being that way."

As soon as the word left Cheryl's lips, the water, in one quick harsh burst, struck Zoey, tossing her into the wet world below them.

She stood up quickly and peeled at the wet cotton that clung to her skin. "Yuck!" she said, grabbing a handful of dirty leaves from her face.

She reared back and threw the muddy junk as far away from their path as she could, but as her body moved to right itself, a rogue wave crashed into her and knocked her down again. But this time, the water had full control over her tiny body as it carried her down the dark grotto.

She broke through the surface, flailing, but her feet couldn't grip the slippery floor.

She tried to swim, but the pull was too strong. She was back under and swirling, alone.

"Zoey!" her parents cried. They ran after her, fighting the resistance of the waves, stumbling and falling themselves.

As she floated beyond the space their flashlights could reach, her voice carried back to them until, eventually, her voice and the sound of the rolling, determined waves became the same.

Cheryl and Eric yelled her name over and over again as they trudged along through the rolling water. Still determined. Still crying. Still shouting. Screaming until their voices were broken and strained.

"Zoey!"

"Zoey!"

"Zoey!"

They passed through tunnel after tunnel and climbed over stacks of soiled rocks.

Their arms bled. Cuts burned across their faces. Still, they pushed ahead.

The water didn't cease in its display of power until they came upon the entrance of an arched passageway.

What the stillness might mean, they didn't care. Together, they trudged through the corridor.

When they reached its end, so, too, came the abrupt conclusion of their quest.

Up ahead, underneath a magnificent glowing waterfall, was their daughter. Alive and playing. And there was something else, too.

It wasn't the sasquatch the two adults doubted even existed; it wasn't that at all. It was something no one, not even Zoey, the biggest believer of them all, could have ever expected.

There, almost so close they could reach out and touch them, was a family of sasquatches.

Frozen, Cheryl and Eric watched as the giant sasquatches leapt and dove—holding hands and laughing, howling and crying. Two of them were fifteen—maybe twenty—feet tall, towering halfway to the lighted waterfall's crest. The few presumably-child sasquatches were already cresting the height of even the tallest of human adults, and each one, no matter its size, had thick, curled, hazel fur that coated its body.

Zoey spotted the bright faces of her parents at the glow's border, swam to the water's edge, and ran up the shining stone path to greet them.

She acted as though she'd lived with the creatures her entire life—and had not, just a few minutes earlier, nearly drowned.

She buried her face in the warm space between her parents and exhaled a long, deep breath.

When she let them go, she took back off, skipping down the trail and leaping into the arms of the smallest sasquatch, who wasn't really *small* at all.

The creature took Zoey to one of the rock cliffs and tossed her into the huge pool. She giggled and squealed as she flew. Truly alive, truly free. After the briefest moment of flight, she smacked the water like a cannonball, only to break through the surface and swim over to the sasquatch just to do the very same thing again.

"Zoey!" Eric whispered in a broken moan, slowly coming out of his trance. He cleared his throat and tried again. Refocused. Charged. This time his voice boomed. "Zoey!"

The sasquatches and Zoey froze as they looked to him, but when he didn't say anything else, they turned back to the waterfall.

Eric spun to his wife. His body shook. "This isn't right, Cheryl. We need to get out of here."

Cheryl laughed quietly, her eyes transfixed by what was in front of her. "They're real," she finally whispered.

"Zoey!" Eric roared. He stomped a few steps down the path. "Now!"

The sasquatches stopped again and, this time, turned to the girl. Although confused by her father's voice, she obeyed as she doggy-paddled to the shore.

The sasquatch who had cast her into the water just a few minutes earlier helped her up and held her hand as they walked away from the waterfall and back toward where her parents stood.

The sasquatch, though, didn't stop when it came upon Cheryl and Eric. Still holding Zoey's hand, it retreated past the archway and into the darkness.

Zoey turned on her light. After a couple of smacks against her hip it shone just as brightly as it had before, and Cheryl and Eric did the same with theirs as they followed behind.

"Zoey," Eric said, softly swatting up ahead at his daughter's free hand. "Let go of that creature."

But Zoey didn't obey her father—not this time.

Even when Cheryl tried the very same thing, Zoey refused her.

"We need to leave," they said. They called their daughter's name, but it was too late. She led them further into the darkness.

The sasquatch took the family to a wall that was so seemingly ordinary. Covered in darkness. Tainted, like all of the others, with splintered dimples from centuries of discordant water droplets.

Drawn on it, brought to life by the luminescence of flashlights, was a map—a map that the sasquatch had drawn of the place it knew and belonged. Its home. Zoey studied how the tunnels connected Wonder Rock's caves and how the woods expanded into the darkness.

The sasquatch bent down and grabbed a piece of chalk from beneath a rock and gave it to Zoey.

The sasquatch pointed from the map of the caves to Zoey. Back and forth. Quickly. Slowly. Searching for a shared language.

Zoey shook her head and rolled her shoulders. "I don't understand," she said.

The sasquatch tried again, taking the chalk and drawing on the map. Something clicked in Zoey.

With the sasquatches' chalk in her hand, she turned to the wall and brought Creekmore to life. The school. The library. The big trees in town. The caves along the southern edge of Wonder Rock. The Cheapies. The couple of roads that brought them together. The trees and field behind her house. Her house. When she finished, she turned to the sasquatch. "Home," she said as she pointed to the map. Then she circled her house and repeated the word. "Home."

The sasquatch howled.

Cheryl walked to her daughter's side and grabbed her hand. "Now let's get to that place you just drew."

"Hang on," Zoey said, pushing away her mother's hand.

"Please," Cheryl said, her voice a whisper.

Zoey turned back to the wall and drew something else. Her arms moved quickly against the wall. In what seemed like no time, she rotated back around and faced the sasquatch. "Zoey," she said. "My name is Zoey."

She pointed from the wall and back to herself. "Zoey," she repeated.

The sasquatch opened its hand to ask if it, too, might use its own chalk, and she obliged, delicately placing the slim stick onto her open palm.

The sasquatch drew a portrait of itself and howled as it patted its chest. This time, its voice sounded different. Clearer and with intent.

"M-maeeeee!" it yelled.

"M-maa-mmaaaaaaaeeeeee!"

It pointed from the drawing to its chest and back again—just as Zoey had done.

"Mae," she said. "Your name is Mae."

Mae smiled at the sound of her name from human lips.

Zoey took Mae's huge, warm hands into her own.

"Zoey!" Cheryl called, her voice louder now. "Zoey!" she repeated. "We need to leave!"

The girl let go of Mae's hands and, instead, full-on embraced her. "I'll be back soon," she said.

Zoey turned and walked toward the light. Her parents followed her, but they took the far side of the cave.

# III

ZOEY BEGGED HER PARENTS TO take her back the next morning. When the request failed, she pleaded that they take a trip to Wonder Rock the next afternoon, and when that plea also went unmet, she kept at it. "We have to go back," she said, sensing their hesitation in not just going back soon, but in going back ever. "I have to. I—I have to."

At night, after she had fallen asleep, Cheryl and Eric stayed up late and discussed how to proceed.

"We should've stopped this years ago."

"We should've, but we didn't."

"There's no way we are going back."

"She's obsessed."

"What if we take her one last time?"

"But isn't that giving in?"

"I don't know what we should do."

"Neither do I."

When Zoey got off the school bus that afternoon, she went in the house and tossed her backpack on the floor. "Daddddd. Mommmm," Zoey sang, walking down the hallway. "Can we go to Wonder Rock? Pretty please. Can we go?"

Still begging, she walked into the living room where Eric was making his way through a set of introductory geography papers that he'd been working on for the past week. She sat down on the carpet in front of him and unclasped her sasquatch pin from her shirt. She held the tiny golden sasquatch against the top of the coffee table and shook it so that it looked like the sasquatch had come to life. "Mr. Eric, sir," she said in a husky, howling voice, "can your daughter come play with me? Please? She'll do extra chores if she has to."

Eric tapped his pen against the paper he was finishing. "Sweetie, you know your mom and I teach, and just in case you've forgotten, you have school yourself. Sasquatch or no sasquatch, we don't have time to go to Wonder Rock during the week. But we will go this weekend one last time. So you can see Mae and say goodbye. Goodbye to her. Goodbye to this whole sasquatch thing once and for all."

Zoey raised her eyebrows. "Goodbye?"

"For forever," Eric said. "Your mother and I are worried about you. We think you need friends and normal interests. We are as much to blame as you for letting this whole weird mess go so far. It's time to grow up—and for all of us to move on."

"But," she said, and then her voice trailed off.

Eric turned back to his papers, and Zoey walked to her room.

# IV

N SATURDAY MORNING, THEY WERE back at the mouth of the cave. "The sun's just now rising. Can't we hang out in the daylight for a couple of minutes?" Eric asked. "Look over the map? Enjoy some light, some hot chocolate? I think I have marshmallows in my bag."

"No," Zoey said, walking past her father without glancing up at him. "I don't need the map, and I'm not wasting a single minute. Drink as you walk."

Cheryl patted Eric's back as she walked past him. "You could be a little more sensitive, you know. And did you really try to beat sasquatches with marshmallows?"

Inside the cave, they followed the same path as before. They knew what to expect. The waves didn't knock them off balance. The slippery floor wasn't quite so slippery. They knew which tunnels to take and which rock piles to avoid.

When they reached the arched passage, Zoey spoke up. "That's the door."

"Certainly not as dramatic an entrance as last time," Cheryl joked.

"Yeah."

They turned corner after corner, with Zoey leading the way, and finally came upon the glowing waterfall. Like before, the glimmering water roared and flowed into the pool below, and the whole place looked as magical and beautiful as it had. But the sasquatches were gone.

"Did we take a wrong turn?" Zoey asked.

"No," Cheryl answered. "This is the place."

They walked further until they were so close to the waterfall that droplets flew from the cascading water and wet their faces.

Zoey cupped her hands and moved them to her mouth. "Mae!" she called. "Mae!"

She repeated her name so many times that the echo swallowed them.

She kicked off her boots and rolled her socks from her feet. Then she sat at the water's border and allowed the cool waves to crash against her legs.

Cheryl went to one side of Zoey and Eric to the other. They followed her lead and sat with their legs draped over the pool's edge.

Cheryl and Eric looked over at one another as they bit their lips.

They sat among the sound of the rolling water for what had to be an hour.

Zoey finally spoke. "I don't understand," she said.

"You found her," Cheryl said. "That's more than anyone else in this entire world can say."

Eric added, "You'll always have that memory. It's time to move on."

Zoey wiped at her face. "Can we just go home?"

"We can," Cheryl and Eric said together.

V

**W**HEN THEY PULLED IN THE driveway, Zoey quickly unlatched her seatbelt and crawled over Cheryl. She hopped out of their still-running truck and ran to their front door.

As Zoey stepped on the porch, Eric turned off the headlights. "This isn't good," Cheryl said. "We need to talk to her."

When they stepped inside, they found their daughter already setting three boxes on the kitchen table.

"What are you doing?" Eric asked.

"I'm getting my desk put back together."

"We thought you were upset," he said.

"I am."

Cheryl spoke. "We understand that, but why are you putting your desk back together? We said today was the last hunt."

"I can't stop looking for her."

"But that was the deal."

"The deal you and Dad made."

"Zoey, it's over. It's time to grow up. Move on. Find other hobbies. Appropriate interests."

"I'm *interested* in sasquatches."

"Zoey!" Cheryl shouted. "Mae and her family are gone. You have to understand that. It doesn't matter how interested in them you are."

"But I will find them again," Zoey said, not looking up and still unpacking her boxes.

Eric ripped the boxes away from his daughter. "Look at us!" His words came broken yet strong. "It's over, Zoey! You found them! It's time to move on!"

Zoey's cheeks grew red. She sat down and finally met the gaze of her mother and father. "I could find them every day, and that still wouldn't be enough. Don't you see that? I wake up thinking about sasquatches, and I go to sleep hoping to dream about them. That's the way it's always been for me. It's the way it's going to keep being for me. You can say what you want, but nothing is going to keep me away from them. I'll go by myself. I'll sleep in the woods. I'll live in caves. I will find them—"

As seemed destined to happen, a familiar howl from outside interrupted them. Zoey didn't stop to even question its origin. She jerked the boxes back from her father's grip, grabbed her flashlight, and took off in the dark.

All night, the girl's parents chased after her. Some say they never stopped.

# WHAT THEY LEFT BEHIND

**A**SH, NOT MANY YEARS FROM entering adulthood, continued with his morning ritual as he had since he'd been trusted to feed himself his own breakfast. Shirtless, he sat on the edge of his bed, stretched his arms above his head, and walked down the hallway to where the soft light from beyond the window barely lit the hard backs of the chairs at the kitchen table. He sat alone and reached inside the chipped porcelain bowl to grab an apple that was past ripeness. As he chewed around the browning spots, he dabbed at the edges of his lips with his open hand, trying his best to contain the fruit's juices. Outside, the moon said goodbye to another night.

Ash's father emerged with daylight and entered the kitchen. Husky and balding, he patted his son's back. After wrestling matches and baseball games, it was the same—the unspoken language they both knew.

As the father began to walk away to find his own nourishment, he turned again to his son.

"What is that?" the father asked, harsher than he intended. His cracked hands pushed, again, harder as they rubbed his son's back.

"Ha ha," Ash said. "I'm a beast, Dad. I told you that you should train with me."

"Yeah, that's not happening," the father said. "I'm serious, though. It feels like there's something on your back."

Ash hugged himself trying to feel. "Are you joking?" he asked.

The father flipped on the light switch and led his son into the hallway to the mirror. "My God," he said. His eyes bulged as he looked, not directly at Ash, but at the boy's unusual reflection.

Ash slowly turned his head to see his image. Instantaneously, whatever sleepiness he possessed vanished. He swatted at his own body. Afraid of who—what—he saw. He spun in circles, bending his arms toward his shoulder blades and slapping at what sprouted from him. "Get them off! Get them off!" he cried.

The father grabbed Ash's arms and held him still. Ash struggled to catch his breath. But the father wrapped his arms around his son. "It's okay. It's okay," he said. He drew his son into his embrace. Ash's breathing slowed.

This was the father's job—to comfort his son.

"Let me look again," the father said, his hands delicately inspecting the boy's skin. Two small, translucent calamuses sprouting pillowy barbs, dug into Ash's back.

"What's going on?" Ash's mother asked, appearing from the darkened hallway.

The father looked into his son's eyes before he spoke. To reassure him. To tell him it would be okay. Then, he grabbed Ash's thick shoulders, and he turned his son so she could gaze upon their boy's back.

She didn't speak. She couldn't. Her hands clutched her lips so tightly that nothing could escape.

"It's wings," the father said.

The doctor looked away when Ash unveiled the pair of unusual wings from under his heavy shirt. But the old man recovered quickly, clearing his throat. "It could be a cancer. Or a benign growth," he said sternly. "Either way, it needs to be removed."

Ash and his parents agreed.

The doctor didn't hesitate when he took a pair of sterilized scissors to the boy's back. He guided the blade into the boy's sallow skin and snapped the thin stems of wing—first under one shoulder and then under the other. The bloodied bundles of budding feathers fell atop the steel operating table and looked like misplaced bouquets of tattered wild orchids.

The doctor was still in the room when a nurse called for him again. "They're returning," the nurse said.

"Sew him up as best you can. We'll wait on the results to know more."

The nurse did as he was told.

The father and the mother didn't cry when the doctor told them the news. They wanted to see Ash.

The doctor led them to his hospital room. "Stay the night if you'd like," he said in a tired voice.

When they opened the door, Ash was asleep, turned on his side. He woke only briefly—to ask how the surgery went, but before they could answer, he was already asleep.

His sprouting new plumes fluttered in the cramped room's manufactured breeze. His bandages were under him, broken apart, on the floor. His scars already invisible.

An apologetic nurse finished tying Ash's left foot to the edge of the bed. "Just in case," she murmured. She grabbed a blue blanket from the closet and placed it on his legs.

The father and mother went to hold their son's hands. "I wouldn't," the nurse said. "He could be contagious."

She met their desperate hands with two bags. "His feathers," she said. "They've been decontaminated."

At the father's first attempt to doze, a pair of frantic voices in the hallway caught his attention. "What did they say?" he asked the mother.

She didn't answer him. Instead, she reached for the television remote. "I'm turning it up," she said.

There were more winged children. Boys and girls. Different ages. From countries all over the world. Canada. Tanzania. Spain. Bolivia. Thailand. Reports updated at the top of each hour. Dozens. Hundreds. Thousands.

The father and the mother wept.

As the sun rose, Ash flew wildly around his room. His wings strengthening and growing at a prodigious pace. The nurse who'd tied him down videoed him when he took flight. "It's for the doctor," she promised.

"Try to calm down, son," the father said, reaching for Ash. "Come on. Try."

Ash was still enough to hover above them—the father and the mother— these two souls whom he loved and loved him in return.

His mouth opened. And closed.

Then, he tried again, but it was no use.

His feathers fell on them, and it was as if they understood what he couldn't find the ability to say.

Before noon, broken farmers seeking the only thing they were capable of loving voiced quick solutions. They offered their empty barns and barren fields. Their containers full of nothingness could not be made alive again. "It's only temporary," they insisted. "Until the kids are back to normal."

They could keep the winged children safe. They could care for them. They could watch over them. Their words, though, broadcast on screens and speakers throughout the world were static variations of blind assurance.

Of course, the powers agreed.

The farms were established before the weekend, with newly ordained "keepers" at the helm. Cleaned troughs and assembled cages shone as the keepers awaited the children.

"We'll keep him indoors," the mother insisted to the nurses and then to the doctors. "He won't burden anyone. He's our son. It's our right," she explained, her voice growing louder with each declaration.

"He will not be going home. Your son isn't *your* son right now," the doctor said.

"But he is. He has always been *our* son," the father interjected.

"You've lost him," the doctor said. Realizing his pitilessness, he corrected himself. "For now," he added.

The keepers went to retrieve Ash first. *Boy 1* the paper said. The father and the mother stood at the entrance to Ash's hospital room door and tried their best to block them.

A cameraman followed behind the keepers. "They're just trying to help," he said.

"Yes. Themselves," the father replied. He stretched his arms from one wall to the other, his legs stout and firm. The mother did the same behind the father.

But they were only stones to be stepped on by the new kings.

The keepers did not speak. Not to the father. Not to the mother. And, when they reached him, not to Ash.

The boy, flying, arched his body toward the men, his wings powerfully rocking the flimsy walls of the room and beating against the window. He looked majestic with his rolling golden wings, already larger than the bed below the boy's body.

His mouth opened. He tried to call. To scream. To cry. Finally, his voice broke through. But it was a new sound, a shriek of otherness that pierced through the entire ward of the hospital, shattered the glass and buckled the tiles beneath him.

As the keepers crouched, the father and the mother raced frantically to their son to clutch him. "Ash!" the mother called. "My boy!" the father followed. But they knew of nothing to tell the boy because they knew of no comfort to utter. They sought to touch him, to calm his heart, but the gloved, cold hands of the keepers stole their embrace.

The keepers unfolded the black tarp tucked under the largest man's arms, and they stretched it across Ash's outspread, beautiful body. His wings fought the heavy sheet, but the men swarmed him.

The spectacular winged boy fell to the ground and succumbed to their power. His feet twitched in submission.

The keepers injected him with a sedative and dragged him down the hallway. His feathers dislodged from his back and littered the floor. "We'll follow the road to our boy," the father said. The mother was already picking up each feather as she went all the way to the fuming truck and its dirty trailer where the cameraman ended his recording.

Two of the men stayed behind and strutted to the desk to sign the papers. Then, they went to the nearby rooms and grabbed the other recently admitted winged children.

The keepers took them all way.

They were the ones, too, who received the praise when, on that initial transport day, only three winged children dissolved into the sun.

---

At the local farm, after he awoke, Ash cradled himself in the back of his dark cage. Morning and night became the same. He didn't want to see the others because he didn't want to see himself.

---

The father and mother bagged Ash's feathers and took them home. They made no distinction in the clean feathers the hospital staff had already given them from the unwashed. They were all priceless relics of the boy who held their joy.

For the keepers, the feathers were a nuisance. Replenishing. Scattering. There was no easy way to contain them.

In the hospitals, they were decontaminated and bagged. Eventually, they were sent away as keepsakes of the past.

But on the farms, it wasn't that easy. The keepers bagged and tied. Bagged and tied. Bagged and tied. Reminders of the present—and indicators of the unknown future. Incinerators arrived, but those contrived fires provided only temporary relief. There were always more feathers no matter how much the keepers swept, gathered, and burned.

———

After the initial week of isolation, the keepers agreed on evening visiting hours. The only time Ash truly came alive was when the father and the mother came to see him, which was every time they were allowed.

During these hours, the keepers unlocked the shiny doors and ushered the physically unchanged inside. "Welcome," they sang. "Enjoy visiting your *children*."

The father and the mother walked among many other families who came with the same purpose.

Although the keepers prescribed specific clothing, few obeyed.

The gray interior sparkled underneath the layers of bleach that permeated the air. Feathers and hay littered the walkway to each cage, which were placed side-by-side along the walls and in the center to form rows.

The farm that held Ash held thousands of winged children in seven barns. "We clean at the top of every hour," one keeper explained, as he walked the facility in his protective attire. "It's an ongoing task." He laughed to himself.

Each time he saw his parents, Ash's wings flapped furiously against the dense metallic walls that enclosed him. He flew to them and rubbed against the bars, their hands petting his ever-growing wings.

The father and the mother cried when they saw the linked chain that wrapped around his foot.

"You are so beautiful," the mother said.

They slipped him apples. He squawked as he tore the flesh from the red fruit and tossed pieces into his mouth.

He put his back to them and flapped furiously again and again throughout the visit, creating a storm of feathers that encircled them.

They picked up each loose fragment of their son, and Ash cawed when they did.

His voice grew louder when they dropped each feather into the bags they'd brought from home.

"If we can't take you, we take what you give us," the father said.

———

After the visitors left, the keepers wheeled the cages into the field, where they allowed the children recess. When they loosened the locks, stretched chains polluted the play yard's packed sky. A pile of cinder blocks polluted the corner of the open space. "Just in case," one of the keepers warned the children.

As their wings buzzed in the warm air, their voices cried loudly creating words that only they could ever know.

Their bodies flew to the peaks of the adolescent pines and then toward the light of the moon. The metal clinked and broke their ascension. Their bodies collapsed to the ground, with their wings still beating. Defeated, but not permanently.

When they gathered their strength, they lifted off the ground again, repeating until morning. Stronger by the hour.

Wars ended. New ones began. The plight of the winged children lost its sensation.

The father and the mother continued to visit. Some of the other most devoted parents did, too. But many who promised love and compassion gave up on their unusual children.

The children, even those without visitors, continued to offer their feathers to anyone who would take them.

It was no surprise when the father and the mother came to visit Ash with their own set of sewn wings, which they draped over their backs. "We got tired of you being the only special one," the mother whispered.

The other visiting families saw the parents' display of affection and mimicked their winged creation.

After a full week of no new diagnoses, the winged children rose with the sun and announced their departure with a synchronized piercing cry. From the keepers employed at the farms to the doctors wondering if their unusual surgeries were over, humans everywhere turned toward the sound.

The cages were broken. The barns were dented. The children were in the sky. Higher and higher. Some still had chains dangling from their legs. With others, it was impossible to tell if they still carried that part of the human world because the feathers clouded the sky and fell like rain.

Many of the humans hid under buildings to keep out of the way.

Ash, leading the winged ones into the sky, looked below one last time. He was curious about what they, these uncompassionate humans, had become. But then he focused on love. It still existed. He knew this because he heard two familiar voices calling beside him. "Ash, our joy. Our beloved boy."

Versions of these stories first appeared in the following publications:

"Those Fantastic Lives" in *Syntax & Salt*
"Losing Light" in *The Cabinet of Heed*
"The Mooneaters" in *Rose Red Review*
"Dolls for the End of the World" in *BULL*
"The Creator" (as originally "The Paper Son") in *Spelk*
"The Galactic Healers" in *Five:2:One*
"Restored" in *Literary Orphans*
"From Hiemslandia" in *Occulum*
"The Comet Seekers" in *Ghost Parachute*
"The Merpod" in *Blind Corner Literary Magazine*
"The Trapper" in *Drunk Monkeys*
"What They Left Behind" in *Crow & Cross Keys*

# ACKNOWLEDGMENTS

**F**OR THE PAST SEVEN YEARS, these stories have filled my life. On certain days, they kept me great company. On other days, they just about broke me. Always, I dreamed of seeing them bound together in a collection. And, now, it's here. There are so many people I must thank for helping to make my dream become a reality.

To my mother, who worked all day at a factory and still came home and opened a book to share with me so I could learn to read, thank you. You've given me so much throughout my life, but this selfless display of love is the one I'm most grateful for.

To Granny, you were the best storyteller a grandson could've asked for. My heart is full of the love with which you spoke, and I still hear your laughter. There are days I need it more than any words can adequately describe.

To Rachel Story, the best teacher I ever had, thank you. You allowed this quiet boy in the back of the room to have a voice. You made me feel strong. You made me feel valued. You made me feel important. A teacher can do nothing greater. I will never be able to thank you enough for giving me the confidence to feel as if I—and my words—mattered. It is because of you that I realized that I had stories within me.

To my many family members—Bear, Nathan, and everyone else—back home, thank you for all of the good memories.

To my second family, including Becky (AKA Suzy Q), Mr. Carr, Nanny, Rog, Becky Hardin, Mckenna, and all the many, many others, thank you for loving and believing in me.

To my friends of old and new, thank you for enriching my life with laughter and joy.

To my special English department colleagues (and friends)—Amelia, Amy, Paula, and Trish—at LHS, thank you for your constant encouragement.

Also, thank you to everyone else at LHS, especially Dr. Jennifer Littleton, for being so supportive of my writing endeavors. Words fail to adequately express my gratitude.

To my students of the past and current, thank you for your goodness. I feel like the future is in good hands with you all leading the way.

To all of the wonderful folks at Queens University of Charlotte, thank you for the constant encouragement. It's a true pleasure of my life to have found such a thoughtful, kind community of lovers of the written word.

To the editors—at *Syntax & Salt, The Cabinet of Heed, Rose Red Review, BULL, Spelk, Five:2:One, Literary Orphans, Occulum, Ghost Parachute, Blind Corner Literary Magazine, Drunk Monkeys,* and *Crow & Cross Keys*—who first gave these stories homes, thank you for championing my work.

To Marti and everyone at City of Light Publishing, thank you for believing in this weird collection of stories and for showing it such love. I am forever grateful for your work and dedication in making this whole incredible journey possible.

To every reader out there, thank you. It's because of you that books continue to exist. What a lonely world it would be without them—and without you.

To Mollie Wobbles, June, Kirby, and Dorchester, you four have shown me what unconditional love is. You've sat on my lap, slept on my shoulders, and scratched at my feet as I wrote these stories. No amount of belly scratches or treats I can offer can repay you for all you've given me. Thank you.

Finally, to Meredith, my wife and best friend, there would be no beginning letter, word, or sentence without your enthusiastic encouragement to chase my dream. So many of these stories are about people searching to understand themselves, the world, and all that is between and beyond. When I found you, I found my light and my guide. For forever and for always, I love you.

# ABOUT THE AUTHOR

**B** RADLEY SIDES' WRITING APPEARS AT *Chapter 16, Chicago Review of Books, Electric Literature, Los Angeles Review of Books, The Millions, The Rumpus,* and *Southern Review of Books.* He holds an MA from the University of North Alabama and is an MFA candidate at Queens University of Charlotte. He lives in Florence, Alabama, with his wife, and he can be found on most days teaching creative writing and English in southern Tennessee. *Those Fantastic Lives* is his debut collection of short stories.

# DISCUSS THIS BOOK

**1.** Which story did you find the deepest connection with and why?

**2.** Sam develops so much as a character throughout "Those Fantastic Lives." It's at the story's end that he finally comes into his own, but his transformation is met with the loss of his grandmother, Nellie. What do you think will happen to Sam? Will he continue to be a psychic?

**3.** Several of the stories involve glowing light. In "Losing Light" there are the fireflies and Gresh's glowing body. The aliens in "The Galactic Healers" arrive on a spaceship that burns "like the setting sun," and in "Restored," Ms. Simone's tears shine in her fountain. What does light offer to these stories and to the collection as a whole? What might it symbolize?

**4.** Told from the perspective of Dean who reflects on the Great Descension from his youth, "Back in Crowville" is a humorous story about human ignorance. Do you think the ghosts ever left Crowville? If so, do you think those humans who left once the ghosts appeared returned?

**5.** Is the mother's action at the end of "The Mooneaters" justified?

6.   Patrick, the protagonist of "Dolls for the End of the World," lives in an abusive home with his father: "His hand flew as if he were a fox and his son's face the prey. Hungry. Vicious. [...] Patrick pulled his hand up and felt the warm sting of his cheeks. The mark would fade just as the others had." Sides clearly paints Patrick's transformation from a timid child into a leader among those who remain in the apocalyptic world, and we are also left with another *possible* transformation: that of Patrick's father. Do you feel any sympathy for the man who is found burned with Patrick's doll "cradled in his charred arms"?

7.   In "What They Left Behind," wings are what cause the separation and imprisonment of Ash and the other winged children, but it's also what gives them the possibility of escaping the cruel world in which they live. Do you see the wings as a blessing or a curse?

8.   In what ways does the title *Those Fantastic Lives* fit this collection?